Manchineel

Felicity Rose Mackinnon

ISBN: 978-1-917293-03-7

The Manchineel is a tropical tree which grows abundantly by the seashore in the West Indies. Golden yellow flowers amid glossy foliage and little apple-like fruits belie its true nature. To eat the apples is fatal. It oozes a sap, a milky fluid that is as caustic as vitriol and poisonous. No-one sits beneath it.

There is a legend that those who sleep beneath it never awaken. Its Spanish name is manzanillo, 'little apple'. The Spanish people call it 'Arbol de la muerte', the tree of death.

Author's Note

This tale of the West Indies is from a very rough draft of my father's, a 'novel' created out of his stint in Barbados in 1912. Turning 'Manchineel' into a proper novel from the largely anecdotal, somewhat disjointed, haphazard set of events that made up his manuscript, which was also full of digressions, has been a labour of love for me and is dedicated to both my late parents. Both, because my patient Mama carefully typed it from my father's dictation. Working out a storyline and a main character from it all, which gave me scope to work with, was great fun. Luckily, he had invented some great characters and dialogue which I have kept true to, as this was of the period. Neither have I added to the facts in the book to keep the integrity of his experiences intact at that significant time.

My dearest Mama had asked me many years ago to 'do something with it dear.' It has taken me a long time to get to it, but here it is at last.

Felicity Mackinnon
Hampshire, 2023

Post Scriptum. In these modern sensitive times, I need to clarify an important factor of colonial West Indian society. There was a very large percentage of mixed blood indicated by European features in its black people. This meant that 'coloured' was an important identification for and of status and mixed blood. The generic word 'black' therefore is inappropriate for the times; then, it was a shade of skin. Thus, the language and views are of those times and are essential for the integrity of the text.

ᴥ Chapter 1 ᴥ

It was a familiar battle of wills. A year ago, he had faced his mother, as now, to tell her that he was off, leaving home, needing a different life. She was outraged then at his going to London. As far as she was concerned it was another planet from their home in Aberdeen and a den of unspeakable iniquity. Now, it was to the other side of the world. He was trying to ignore the fright he knew he had given her as she glared her challenge at his news. He smiled winningly down at her hoping he could soothe her with his considerable charm. He was not fond of confrontation.

'But mother, it's 1912 and the age of steam! The 'Magdalena' is a Steam Packet not a sailing boat! There really is nothing to worry about.'

His mother, drawn up to her full five foot two inches, hands clasped tightly across her stout corseted middle, was rigid with rage. His news, his need to leave again and then his conceit that he could charm her over-rode her fear for him. She knew bitterly that she was impotent to stop him but she threw every blistering argument at him she could think of as to the folly, the dangers, the diseases and worst of all, the foreign-ness of it.

He countered them all with sweet reasonableness. He assured her that Barbados may be the other side of the globe but it was a delightfully civilized British Colony.

Also, he was going to a highly respectable job in a Bank which was going to accommodate him to boot, so what was there to worry about?

She raged at his extreme youth. Rubbish, he was 22 and already seasoned by his sojourn in London. He was quite capable of looking out for himself.

She scoffed at that and tried the tactic of her advancing years. To no avail. His passage was booked. It was a *fait accompli.* Mrs MacNeil was defeated. Sandy was going: to work in the British West Indian Bank in Barbados.

❧

Sandy's eyes re-focused onto the ceiling of the stuffy cabin where he lay on his bunk, hands tucked behind his head, chuckling as he lay remembering his mother's scornful animadversions and grumblings. These she had kept up in some form right up to the last. Their views on the potential of such a venture were never going to coincide. He had resolutely insisted that neither she nor his father come down to see him off and had blithely gone off alone to board the ship in peace. He was doubly glad she hadn't seen the vessel he was setting out in.

The 'Magdalena' was actually rigged for sail as well as steam and would not have reassured his mother in the least. And what an old tub she had turned out to be! Royal Mail Steam packet sounded impressive but she was still a tub. Though she rolled and pitched even when there was no evident reason for her doing so, he revelled in it. In fact, the more she rolled and pitched like a bucket, the better he liked it. She was his first ship and he'd never before been to sea: her novelty and eccentricities gratified his boyish fancies.

To Sandy's delight, he took to the sea like a born sailor and went up on deck as often as he could. He would lean over the rail, the wind whipping his thick fair hair about his uncovered head, his hazel eyes gleaming with relish as he exhilarated in the sight and smell of the grey-green seas the doughty ship ploughed through. The deeper the troughs and the more spume on the wave tops, the more he loved it.

In fact, being up on deck in the invigorating sea air suited Sandy very well. The two cabin companions assigned to his berth, Leach and Joyner, turned out to be a singularly glum pair. They were also fellow-employees of the Bank he was to work in, in Bridgetown, Barbados. They were thoroughly miserable about being aboard, being at sea and setting off for parts unknown, so Sandy was only too pleased to leave them to it.

They were all three much the same age. To Sandy's eye, Leach and Joyner, with their unhealthy vaguely bleached look, were the personification of office clerks wan from working long hours indoors. To his faint disgust neither had any inclination for a bracing walk on deck or interest in the ship. He privately stigmatised them as a colourless couple of chumps devoid of both looks and personality. A pigeon pair in fact. Both were dark haired, non-descript of eye and pasty complexioned; Leach's was especially bad.

Looking at Sandy's bright head and healthy out-door skin was an affront to them both so they were only too happy to do without his company. They had no appreciation of the facetious remarks with which he tried to enliven their dim view of things either. Since the cabin they all occupied was rather cramped, his absences were a considerable relief on all points.

As the 'Magdelena' sailed south and entered the Bay of Biscay he thanked his lucky stars that he had turned out to be a good sailor, for fully in keeping with the Bay's treacherous reputation, the weather was atrocious. The 'Magdalena's' immediate response to the wildly heaving seas and fierce winds was of course to wallow and buck even more. The effect on the passengers was equally immediate and started a virtual *en masse* exodus as they hurriedly sought the privacy of their cabins. Leach and Joyner had barely left theirs since boarding and it was no surprise to Sandy that they were both prostrated with sea-sickness. In a very short space of time the ship appeared deserted.

Sandy and a young Canadian, equally free of sea-sickness or fear, found they were the only ones left on their

3

feet, barring the senior deck Officers. Undismayed, they'd had the ship to themselves and thoroughly enjoyed the emptiness of the public rooms, the wind-swept deck and the unrestrained wildness of both weather and ship. Naturally high-spirited, they revelled in the freedom and just being able to please themselves.

Now and then they saw a pallid passenger making a brief visit to a corner of the dining room to attempt a meal. However, the sad invalid soon stumbled off back to their cabin, their agony wholly unrelieved by their endeavour to assuage their digestive tract with food. Sandy and pal meanwhile, ate on with relish and enjoyment.

After a few days, when the 'Magdalena' had reached calmer waters and a warmer clime, the recovering passengers began to appear on deck. To the healthy, irrepressible Sandy, a sorry crowd they looked as they emerged from the bowels of the ship, pasty-faced and hollow-eyed, resembling, he thought, the inmates of a sanatorium. It was surprising however, what a day or two in quiet waters did for them. Sandy observed them with amusement and some irony. He noted wryly that they very quickly returned to normal, forming themselves into cliques; civil servants being uncivil to those in trade, while French West Indians and Mulattos were cut by all and sundry. He found all the shifts and groupings very entertaining and quietly enjoyed his own cynicism.

As they sailed south Sandy settled into a contented pattern of easy pleasure. He spent his days either burning off some energy playing deck games or, lulled by the rhythm of the ship, lounging in the sun or his cabin, if it was free, after a good meal. The southerly seas also brought further diversions; dolphins and flying fish flashing and leaping alongside the ship, the water sparkling off their lithe bodies. He loved leaning over the ship's rail watching them.

Often, he saw great masses of weed from the Sargasso Sea and Portuguese Men O'War sailing along like translucent ships below the surface. He was in his element enjoying the sweet freshness of the sea air, the warmth of the sun and especially how it added a glitter and sheen to the rich blue-green of the seas rolling away to the horizon. To him it was all pure hedonism.

Meanwhile Sandy's cabin companions and colleagues Leach and Joyner, were not enjoying the voyage. They were thoroughly disagreeable, being sea-sick for the greater part of the voyage and for the rest, moaning about the food, the smells on the ship and constantly expressing doubts as to the wisdom of going to this foreign country at all. They found Sandy's *joie de vivre* and abounding good health an additional offence. Many rude remarks were uttered such as 'Bloody Scotchmen making great pioneers as they were so glad to leave their own rotten country.' Seeing them prostrate on their bunks gazing at him with loathing in their lack-lustre eyes he tried to cheer them up with descriptions of the dolphins leaping through the bounding waves or the lovely roast chicken he'd had for dinner. He was glaringly admonished to go to hell and drown himself.

His afternoon siesta was suddenly interrupted by the cabin door being jerked open. His young Canadian pal stuck his head through the aperture.

'Hey Mac! We've just sighted Barbados!'

Sandy swung his feet over the edge of the bunk and jumping to the floor dashed up on deck after his friend. He hurried to the guard rail full of anticipation. All there was to see however, was a rather disappointing hazy smudge on the horizon. He gazed at it with shaded eyes.

'How long d'you think it'll take us to make it to Port? Can't wait to get ashore and see what's in the offing!'

'Haven't an earthly chum,' said his companion. 'Ages yet I expect in this old girl.'

5

Sandy grinned. He was going to miss being rocked to sleep by the dear old tub when they got to land. But he was certainly eager to discover what life had to offer in Barbados at last.

'I'd better shoot off and pack before my loveable colleagues sully the cabin with their godawful presence!' he said. There certainly wasn't much in view yet. By the time he'd finished packing his gear he hoped there would be decidedly more to see.

It was late afternoon by the time they were close enough to make out the island. It looked serenely beautiful as the sun was going down. Brilliant green, with dark shadows flying across the plantations, palm tree swaying in the wind, long stretches of glorious sandy beaches, coral reefs being pounded by the surf, and of all things, windmills dotted over the landscape. He was suddenly impatient to be on land and explore everything, to soak up the colour and ripe greenness. The cold granite and subdued colours of his northern home seemed infinitely far away.

They anchored out in the roadstead. The inner harbour, known as The Careenage did not have enough depth of water for any but small ships such as schooners, sloops and the like.

The Port doctor came aboard to give them a clean bill of health. His launch was followed by crowds of shore boats filled to overflowing with goods, their vociferous owners yelling for custom in a virtual babel of undistinguishable sound. Bumping and shoving each other to get near the gangway they surged around the ship and gangway completely unconcerned at the possibility of capsizing. Numbers of small boys, in all manner of primitive craft added to the racket by bawling for silver to be thrown into the water for which they dived and fought under water, their brown bodies as supple as eels. Repeatedly clambering agilely aboard their frail little craft, they stood up, dripping and grinning happily, and yelled for more.

Sandy had never seen anything like it. In the cacophony it was impossible to distinguish much in the dialect being roared up to the ship's passengers milling around at the rails. He was too engrossed to notice whether they too were enjoying this extraordinary welcome as much as he was.

As he was viewing this lively and exotic scene with deep interest and satisfaction, the Steward came up to tell him that a gentleman from the West Indian Bank had arrived to take him, Leach and Joyner ashore. The reminder that this was not just a pleasure trip cut through his rapt attention. As from tomorrow he would be a junior employee of the West Indian Bank, Barbados branch. Undeterred however, he went below to the cabin where Leach and Joyner were already talking to their visitor. He introduced himself as a Mr Williams and was none other than the Chief Cashier.

It became apparent that he had been trying to cheer up Sandy's colleagues and was reassuring them that they'd enjoy it alright once they'd settled down, but they were looking thoroughly miserable and as despondent as ever. This mood was not improved when they found that they were all expected to part with two gold sovereigns each to the Steward for what he didn't do for them on the voyage. Leach and Joyner couldn't let that go without complaint. They viewed it as rank extortion and for once Sandy agreed with them.

Soon however, their luggage was manhandled down the gangway into a shore boat. As they were rowed ashore, Sandy, now right in the midst of the lively scene, absorbed it all the more with huge enjoyment, oblivious of his two companions' stolid silence. The Careenage was alive with movement. Rowing boats, bumboats, lighters, launches and even small yachts moved about with much shouting and gesticulating from their crews. From the wharf a positive crescendo of sound smote his ears, mostly from Negroes loading goods and barrels onto long lines of schooners.

These schooners moored in lines alongside the wharves were packed so closely together that the bows of one touched the stern of another. They were so exactly from a century or so before, looked so completely unchanged, that they could not fail to enthral Sandy mused, taking it all in. The very name Careenage was so evocative of pirates coming in to careen their vessels between voyages; of Captain Teach and the Spanish Main. He felt it would have been perfectly in keeping if the present crews looked the part, complete with earrings and cutlasses flashing in the sun. He laughed at himself for a romantic chump. But everything meeting his fascinated gaze seemed so much larger than life and utterly unlike anything he had encountered before.

'I say, this is fully up to expectations!' he remarked as they stepped ashore, revelling in the strangeness and bustle and clamour on the wharf and looking about him with interest. The sweet smell of molasses and other spicy odours came from the open dockside warehouses and hung in the warm air. Sandy sniffed it appreciatively. Not so his colleagues. Although relieved to be on *terra firma* at last, the spicy perfume was a bloody stink and the niggers awful, was their reply.

Even as their luggage was landed, the dust and noise and shouting rapidly subsided. Warehouse doors closed, natives moved off and disappeared in moments. The change was unexpected, strange, abrupt. Lights gleamed suddenly. It was as if one switch had been thrown and another put on as the night came down like a knife. They had to stand for a moment to adjust to the sudden dark and silence.

'Sundown comes quickly in Barbados,' remarked Mr Williams rather unnecessarily. 'It happens in this part of the world. This way' he said and led the way towards a narrow iron gate almost abutting onto the wharf. They passed a great securely locked and chained double iron gate on the wharf itself. It was only used, Mr Williams told them, when bullion was being transferred. Their gate led off a narrow lane. This, their host pointed out, went from the wharf to the main street, Broad Street; a complete misnomer as it turned out.

'The Bank closed some time ago. This will be your entrance. Your quarters are over the Bank itself,' he said leading them through the gate.

A Negro appeared carrying a lantern. 'Here Theo,' Mr Williams said, 'show these gentlemen to their rooms and get them something to eat.' Mr Williams turned to the three young men. 'I must push off now. I'll leave you to the tender mercies of Theo here. I have a long way to go to get home. I live about two miles out of town but I'll see you in the morning. Goodnight,' and left them to it.

'Don't think much of that fellow!' said Joyner, scowling indignantly. 'He might have had the decency to ask us to his house for dinner seeing we're strangers in a foreign land!'

'You two are a pair of chumps,' Sandy said. 'Why would he want your miserable mugs at his dinner table?'

'Come dis way, Gen'man, please,' said Theo, a perfectly black man but with European features and dressed in a non-too-clean white drill suit.

Without more ado, Sandy followed Theo as he led the way from the gate. Leach and Joyner followed, muttering and still full of a sense of ill-usage. The Bank, dimly seen as they approached from the gateway appeared to be a large stone building of three stories. It had a bare paved courtyard surrounded by high stone walls. The stark contrast of the prison-like aspect of the place to their colourful reception and exotic sights at the Careenage was striking. Sandy felt a sudden keen disappointment; that life was going to be ordinary after all.

Entering the building, they followed Theo up the uncarpeted stairs and through some large dusty rooms, their heels echoing hollowly as they walked over wooden floorboards destitute of either rugs or lino. In fact, the Bank it appeared, like most wealthy concerns, adopted a cheese-paring attitude in anything relative to their employees. Not by any stretch of the imagination could it be said that their quarters were luxuriously furnished. They seemed completely devoid of any comfort.

Their three bedrooms on the top floor had more than sufficient cubic feet but that was about all, barring the absolute basics. Viewing the one allotted to him with some dismay, Sandy found that the furniture consisted of a black iron bedstead complete with mosquito curtain, one cane-bottomed chair, a dilapidated washstand bearing a non-descript red earthenware jug and basin and a dirty cupboard redolent of mildew. He looked about him with a sinking heart. Even his natural ebullience was dimmed.

The spartan welcome of these rooms had an even more dampening effect on the other two, so with very little ceremony, they dumped their bags and went down to see if the lounge on the second floor offered any relief from all this desolation.

The word lounge, they discovered, was a euphemism. All three looked around in consternation. It contained a tattered hammock slung between two pillars, a couple of dirty tables and a few derelict chairs, two being of the type known as 'Berbice.' These had extensions so one could rest with the legs outstretched. Not that they were a concession to comfort in the room, they were merely typical local furniture. The sheer size of the room made the contents even more disreputable, seedy and forlorn.

There were two other rooms on the same floor, large, very dusty and totally devoid of furniture. They served only to add to the air of decay and depression of the rest of the building. Sandy, Joyner and Leach all surveyed their new home with dismay and sat silent and despondent in the ghastly lounge each occupied with their own thoughts, no doubt longingly of Home Sweet Home, and all its far too distant consolations.

Sandy, bored with the pervading gloom got up and strolling around noticed that the dismal lounge had one compensating feature. A large verandah ran the width of the building, giving a glorious view of the careenage and roadstead. It extended out some feet over the courtyard below so he hauled over one of the Berbice chairs and making himself comfortable, stretched out his legs, relaxed and admired the scene below in the harbour, and ignored the other two. Leach was actually in tears. After a while he stopped snivelling and suddenly shouted,

'I'm hungry! - Where's that nigger?'

'Ring the bell,' advised Joyner.

'Can't see a bell.' said Sandy. 'Don't they clap their hands or something in the tropics?' They clapped their hands in the approved manner without result.

'Why not try the Russian method' said Leach, who was getting riled. 'I had an uncle in Russia who said the best way for getting prompt service was to smash something.' He jumped up and grabbed a hideous vase of considerable size and threw the thing over the balcony where it crashed onto the stone courtyard below.

Almost at once Theo appeared at the door.

'Cud deah! Sah, what you tink you doin? Yo caint trow de tings out de windah!'

'Here nigger,' said Leach. 'Get a move on and bring in the grub!'

The Negro walked slowly and with great dignity across the room and looked at Leach with a touch of censure in his dark eyes.

'Gen'men, I re-fuse to be called niggah. I be a British citizen. You new heah and doan understan'. I do my job foh

11

you and doan make trouble, but yo' must not call me niggah.' He turned and went back through the door.

A bleak silence fell.

In a short while, Theo emerged carrying a large steaming platter of what proved to be delicious flying fish along with a pot of excellent coffee. Leach had the grace to look uncomfortable.

When the meal was cleared away, Sandy decided to speak up.

'Look here you two, on board while you were rendering the cabin unspeakable, I found a history of the West Indies. I did some reading up and let me tell you the native West Indian, especially the Barbadian, regards himself as a Britisher and not at all subservient. He is a British Citizen and proud of it, his flag is the Union Jack and King George is his King, - so I think Leach, you'd be as well to treat Theo as a manservant, not as a menial. And hold your tongue about niggers,' he added.

Leach didn't answer. He just slumped in his chair looking the picture of gloom; his mood amply expressed on the pasty oval of his pimply face. This was not improved by his dark hair being plastered to his head with the pungent pomade he favoured. Sandy viewed him with some contempt. Being bigoted and narrow was not entirely uncommon, but Leach was a miserable self-pitying blighter and a lazy one to boot as his slack body testified.

Joyner meanwhile was sitting bolt upright in his chair for all the world as if he was waiting any minute for something to happen. He didn't endear himself much to Sandy either. His bland and rather babyish face with its pale eyes seemed to reflect his entire character. Also, he was a follower. Worse still, he followed Leach of all people! What a pair of fatheads to be working with! He hoped they were going to buck up once they'd got into the swing of things here.

He shrugged off his thoughts and strolling over to the verandah, savoured the night air.

'What are you two chaps going to do now?' he asked over his shoulder. Both expressed an earnest desire to go to bed. They were bored, fed up and tired and didn't think they were going to like the tropics.

'Come on,' said Sandy ignoring this craven stuff. 'One of those empty rooms looks over the main street so let's have a look and see what the town's like,' he urged. Grudgingly they followed him to one of the bare rooms. Leading them across the dusty floor to the window, Sandy flung it open and they looked down at the scene below. The street was thronged with people and lights flickered everywhere. Sandy's eager eye took it all in. To him it was exotic and full of interest, but by the looks on their faces, faintly terrifying to the other two.

'I'm going out to see the town.'

'What?' exclaimed Leach. 'At this time of night? You'll probably get your throat cut!'

'I say MacNeil! You can't mean it?' added Joyner. 'Won't you get lost or something?'

'It's only ten o'clock and the town looks lively enough. You two kill-joys can do as you like,' he said, giving up on the pair of them. 'In any case anything's preferable to your ugly mugs. I'm going to change.'

Turning on his heel he strode off cheerfully to his room leaving the others to enjoy their miseries together. He hurriedly changed into a lounge suit and in minutes, was dashing down the stairs, and was out through the side gate and up into Broad Street.

There he joined the strolling Barbadians in the busy roadway. The night air struck chilly after the heat of the day, but in no time, he hardly noticed it. He looked about him with eager curiosity.

A dense throng promenaded the well-lit thoroughfare. This was due partly to gas-light but more so to the numerous candles and paraffin lamps of the native hucksters, Negro women clad in white starched dresses. They stood with their trays of fruit, vegetables or cheap goods balanced across one muscular thigh and maintained by the foot resting on a box, the other sturdy leg taking the weight. With their shiny fat faces topped by turbans of brilliant hue and spotless white muslin frocks with the appropriate colourful reef around their ample waists, they were the most picturesque street vendors Sandy had ever seen.

There were no pavements, so the Barbadians strolled aimlessly about talking and gossiping, some with guitars and singing, while others lounged in groups good-naturedly arguing the toss. The men-folk were either in the ragged shirt and trousers of plantation workers, in bare feet with calloused soles so thick that they could have trodden on broken glass without harm, or flashily dressed, mostly in loud patterned American suits and knobbly-toed shoes which they wore with great panache and satisfaction. There was constant movement and noisy activity.

While it was all enthralling and different, Sandy found it a little disconcerting all the same to be surrounded by so many coloured faces ranging from deepest ebony to milk chocolate with very few white faces to be seen.

He made a brief survey of the town, a few streets of mean two-storied houses and several more pretentious stone buildings, but he soon went back to Broad Street where he hoped there was some fun to be had. The chemist, or 'Doctor's Shop' as it was called, seemed to be a favourite rendezvous. It was crowded, but more with loungers than customers, he noted. He was delighted to be able to buy a cigar there for only a few coppers. This was decidedly promising.

Entering the street once more he passed quite a number of bars, but they looked too forbidding for him to tackle so he strolled on enjoying his cigar. He came to a fair-sized hotel with a large wooden verandah and was surprised and gratified to find that it was The Ice House mentioned by Arnold Bennett in one of his novels. This was more like it, he thought. He went in and sat down and ordered a cold beer. He was immediately joined by a well-dressed chap who looked to be in his twenties. He introduced himself as the House Surgeon at the local hospital. Pyle was his name he said.

'How d'you do!' said Sandy smiling and offering his hand. 'I'm MacNeil. Sandy, short for Alexander. I'm at the Bank.'

'Right. Richard.' he grinned. 'What could be better - a tropic night and a cold beer!'

Pyle turned out to be a local boy and after being educated at Codrington College, Barbados' own college, he went to England to Durham University to which it was affiliated and took his medical degree over there. He spoke affectionately and enthusiastically of his time there. Sandy filled him in on the necessary about himself, adding that his own father was a doctor back in Aberdeen. They were on the friendliest terms from the word go. He could hardly believe his luck.

'My father has a yacht. We could go yacht-racing one day if you like. There's a lot of fun to be had on the Island one way or another. The Bajans are a hospitable lot and take kindly to people from 'home' - that's what we call England though we are born and bred here and call ourselves Bajans!'

'Well, I'm enjoying every minute, I must say!' said Sandy. 'I don't intend to stay a minute longer than necessary in that barren dump over the Bank so I'll be ready for any high jinks that are on offer!' He tossed off the last of his beer and set off with his easy-going companion as far as the hospital.

They walked across a square amazingly called Trafalgar Square which to his astonishment was even complete with

15

a life-size statue of Nelson. Sandy was highly diverted at finding the square named after London's famous landmark with England's beloved hero himself in this tropical setting. Pyle told him of the Bajan's pride that the great man had visited them just before Trafalgar and their statue went up thirty years before the London one. They passed a bridge over the harbour named after Joseph Chamberlain which led his companion said, to the suburbs of Worthing and Hastings a few miles along the coast road and worth a visit for their beaches.

'Look out for the coral dust though old chap. It comes off the roads in a cloud you'll find. Regrettably in this island, it carries the tetanus bacillus so if you even scratch yourself get it seen to pronto and get over to us straight away for an anti-tetanus injection - I mean it! It's a nasty death! It thrives in the cane plantations so we see some bad cases. Otherwise, it's a healthy enough place,' he added reassuringly.

Assuring his new medical friend of taking due note of this advice, they arrived at the hospital. Sandy thanked Pyle and left with his promise to see him in the very near future.

Feeling very pleased with his first night ashore, Sandy set off to walk back to the Bank relishing the soft night air and the blaze of bright starlight that illumined the way. The boats snubbed sleepily at their moorings and the only sound was the water slapping gently against the wharf-side. All was serene as he walked along by the Careenage. Once again, he turned into the lane and entered the narrow iron gate to the Bank. By the time he climbed the stairs and made his way upstairs, all he could think of was bed; he was too tired by that time to be bothered by his dingy and cheerless surroundings.

✵ Chapter 2 ✵

Bridgetown woke early. Just after sun-up in fact. An incredible hub-bub shattered Sandy's slumbers and since it showed no signs of abating, he got up and went down in his dressing gown to the verandah to get a proper view of what it was all about.

The Schooners immediately drew his attention. All around them seethed with vociferous activity. They were in the lively process of being loaded. Mule-driven lorries piled with great barrels of molasses swarmed with natives who were in the process of man-handling the great barrels down on to the wharf. They did this with amazing ease and much yelling. The noise was tremendous.

His fascinated eyes then saw that these hogsheads of molasses were being slung between two large iron-shod wheels on a strange looking contraption which was operated by the Negro loaders for transfer to the ship. This extraordinary method, Sandy saw, was that the Negroes pushed this spider-like monstrosity along at great speed and then, as it gathered momentum, jumped onto the vehicle so that their combined weight caused it to career along at break-neck speed. Then it braked suddenly as the ship's side was reached. It looked dangerously erratic. It turned out that it was actually called a 'spider' and accidents were appallingly frequent. It would over-turn often pinning a Negro underneath, or the brakes failed and it hit the ship's side, or the erratic steering caused collisions with other vehicles.

This amazing performance was accompanied by more yells and raucous instructions from one native to another as the barrels were delivered and hauled aboard. The dust and racket were being added to by mule-drawn trams and numerous horse-drawn buggies whose drivers were all actually making their way somehow through the bustle of the crowded wharf. Over all was a clattering cacophony from chains, pulleys and derricks. The drive and vitality of the place were vividly apparent in the hurly-burly toiling, shouting and constant movement everywhere he looked. This is a noisy little town alright thought Sandy.

At a very light breakfast served by a very glum-looking Theo, an equally glum Leach and Joyner made very little conversation so Sandy was left in peace. That done, they went downstairs and entered the Bank to be met by the Chief Cashier.

His first job, Sandy was pleased to find, was to go round the town to certain addresses with Bills of Lading for signature. Eager to see things by daylight, he set off in his new palm beach suit full of the joys of spring and a straw hat shading his hazel eyes.

He stepped out onto the wharf and was met now by a scene drawn plainly from the time of the Pharaohs. An unending stream of black women, clad entirely in white dresses reaching to their ankles, and chanting a long-drawn out working song, were carrying baskets of coal on their heads. The procession led from an enormous coal dump some two hundred yards from the wharf to several huge black barges tied up to the wharf itself. Intrigued and amazed, he saw the women arrive at the barges and without a pause they heaved the coal from the baskets into the barge hold and then seamlessly joined the return cavalcade to the fuel dump, a continuous unending chain of human beings. Carrying coal in white dresses! Did that and the singing mitigate the ghastly dusty and monotonous job he wondered? He had his doubts. He was both appalled and fascinated.

As the barges were filled, Negroes cast off the mooring ropes and, with one man at the stern and another at the bows, they rowed the heavy barges with immensely long sweeps, or oars, far out to the ships waiting out in the roadstead. When re-counting this to his new medical friend Richard Pyle later, he was told that the average life of these bargees was tragically brief. The strain of wielding these long sweeps on a diet consisting mainly of rum contributed largely to their deaths. As for the coal procession, it went on from morn to night all through the year.

Turning aside from this disturbing though enthralling scene, Sandy continued on his way. Just as the wharf was noisy and busy so was the town. The atmosphere here though was one of lively enjoyment and good humour and this soon dispelled his uneasiness over the arduous toiling of the women on the wharf.

The streets were thronged with people laughing and talking, and mule-driven trams, buggies and bicycles added considerably to the dust raised by the many feet. The stores and bars were doing a roaring trade and the smiling faces and shining teeth and evident good humour of even the most ragged, and there were plenty of these, exhilarated him afresh. The hot sun, the ebullient life and cosmic quality of it all made Sandy sure he was going to like it here. Throughout the day, in the warehouses and offices, he met friendly white Bajans who seemed genuinely glad to meet a man from England and many were the meetings he promised to keep.

His first working day therefore was pleasant and unexacting. He spent it chiefly away from the Bank on the various errands he was only too happy to be given. It naturally suited him down to the ground to be outside and getting about the place. He hoped there would be frequent errands like this for the Bank. It gave him a perfect opportunity to explore and find his way about the town. To someone of his extrovert nature and with his insatiable curiosity for people and places, it was manna from Heaven. The sun beating onto his shoulders through his jacket, the exotic quality of the sights, noise and vigour of the surging humanity on the streets were in such contrast to his year's experience in London and especially his own home town of Aberdeen. He felt he couldn't get enough of it. As he went about the town to his various destinations, straw hat at a jaunty angle he felt himself fortune's favourite indeed.

❧

When night came, he was determined to see Bridgetown's life after dark again. As soon as he had dined, and impeccably dressed as usual, he made for The Doctor's Shop. He was selecting a cigar when a big gaily-clad black man took a handful of more expensive cigars from another box and threw the assistant a five-dollar note. He then handed the cigars to Sandy with a huge smile.

'Hey I say, you can't do that!' Sandy cried, a good deal astonished.

'Oh yes I can sah, if yo pardon de liberty. Allow me to introduce myself. Leo Ferguson. My brother Theo's your servant an he tell me to look after you Mistah Mac. He like you sah, but he not so shua 'bout your frien's, de other gen'man.'

'Ferguson!' said Sandy with a laugh, 'Another Scotsman!'

'Yes sah. Far back we have some Scotchman in our family my father tol' me,' said Leo happily. 'I'm a man of de world sah. I work on Panama Chain, on de canal. I see many die, but I no die. When I save money, I say to dem Americano, Maan, I doan want to die, gie me my money, I get back to my country, I'm British. No more work for dem Americano and I leave sah, an come home to Barbad's.'

Leo was a powerfully built young man and didn't need the padding of his natty American suit to emphasise his shoulders. His suit was blue with a white stripe and his baggy trousers fell in neat folds over his bright yellow shoes. His hat was white with a broad brim dashingly completed with an underlining of bright green. His whole get-up was striking to say the least and Leo seemed well-satisfied with his appearance. His dark face gleamed with gratification. Some of his teeth were gold-filled. Not, he explained because they were decayed but just to show he was a man of means.

Sandy accepted the cigars with alacrity and offered Leo one. They lit up and strolled into Broad Street.

'Now sah, where would you like to go?'

'Let's go and have a drink.'

'Sure,' said Leo, 'but we cain't go to some classy hotel. Some white folks doan like coloured gen'man, even when dey have plenty dollars.'

'I don't want a classy hotel!' protested Sandy. 'I want to see life, with music and dancing and girls!'

'O.K. I show you de place, only Mistah Mac, promise me you doan go 'way with any woo-man unless I tell you she alright for nice gen'man.'

'Right.' he agreed.

Leo led the way off the main thoroughfare and after passing through some mean streets, they suddenly came upon a building blazing with lights and noise.

'The Flag Hotel!' announced Leo proudly. 'A very select place!'

The ground floor of The Flag was open to the four winds where hordes of tatterdemalion Negroes of both sexes were milling around a bar counter, yelling and gesticulating with great exuberance in their own very individual manner. The noise, accompanied by the pungent musky smell of pressed humanity that flowed from within was almost overpowering. Sandy hesitated at this spectacle but Leo reassured him.

'Sah, we go upstairs where we doan associate wid dem black niggah trash.'

He led the way to an upper storey which sported a verandah supported by iron pillars from the street below.

This, Leo said, was for the better dressed saloon bar class. There were more hordes of merrymakers on this storey, but here at least, they were seated at tables and although creating almost as much row as those below, their gestures and exhortations were marginally more restrained. Even dance music could be heard.

Leo shooed two indignant white girls from a table, telling them to give way for the new English Bank man. They replied by upbraiding Leo as a fugitive from the Panama Chain. They didn't mind giving up their seats to that white boy, but 'what the hell?' Sandy made his peace by inviting the ladies to join them at the table and have a drink. Leo looked discomfited and muttered something about 'poor white trash' and 'red legs'.

The girls, both pretty, with European features and clear white complexions, interested Sandy. They looked to be no more than 18 years old and were dressed very becomingly in smart white lace frocks with their glossy black hair done up in rolls on their foreheads and long curls at the back. He wondered what they were doing in a dive like this. They introduced themselves as sisters, Jennie and Sadie and considerably mollified, sat down at the table.

Leo attracted the attention of a huge Negro acting as waiter and ordered two rum swizzles 'foh the gen'man' an two scotches for de ladies.'

Savouring his drink, Sandy grinned amiably at the two girls before him and Leo unbent at last and told him that their lady friends were not in this establishment from choice, an unkind fate was responsible. Their ancestors were Scotch or Irish criminals deported from Britain in Cromwellian times and they rightly refused, said Leo, to work in the fields like common blacks or engage in low class jobs like shop girls. They preferred to be ladies of leisure. In any case it was easier money.

'But why call the Scotch 'red legs?' queried Sandy.

'Aah, dem Scotch,' replied Leo, and launched into a colourful story of the Scots arriving in the islands off the boats from England in the 17th century wearing their kilts and their legs being burnt red by the unaccustomed tropic sun.

Sandy had a sudden vivid mental picture of these sad, scorched, bare-legged Scots.

'Leo, where did you learn all this?'

'Sah, I was a student at Codrington College. Dat's where I learnt all 'bout dem Cromwellian criminals.'

'Well don't you believe that!' Sandy cried. 'They were political martyrs. Some were men of position, professional men, country gentlemen and others who detested Cromwell and all his works, so for all you know these charming guests of ours may be descendants of some of the best blood in Scotland!' Sandy gestured as if toasting his martyred countrymen and drained his glass with enthusiasm.

'Cud deah!' exclaimed Jennie. 'Tell us some more! Bank man, you nice boy! Like to sleep with me tonight, eh?' She smiled invitingly at him revealing her pretty white teeth and tapping them with her whisky glass.

'Lay off Jennie,' growled Leo. 'Dis boy in my charge, he aint goin' sleepin' wid any woo-man yet awhile!' He gestured to a perspiring waiter for more drinks.

Sandy felt his control slipping somewhat. These rum swizzles are insidious things, he thought.

'What's in these things?' he asked, holding up a fresh drink to the light and admiring its pinkish tint and the slight froth at the top.

'One of sour, two of sweet, three of strong and four of weak' chanted Leo. 'De sour's fresh lime juice, de sweet's syrup, de strong's rum and de weak is crushed ice. You put de whole lot in a tumbler wid a good dash of angostura bitters and swizzle it wid a 'swizzle stick.' Barbados, he said with a grin, even supplied the bush with the swizzle stick practically ready made. It was a twig, he explained, with a few little twigs growing out like a fan at one end which you plunged into the drink and twirled it between the palms of the hands.

'Perfect! Everything to order! Lovely stuff,' smiled Sandy happily.

'It's a musical drink too!' added Sadie. 'You can hear de froth singin' if you put it to your eah!'

'You always know you had enough if you cain't hear de froth singin' for de singin' in yo own eahs!' said Leo with a happy grin. After about four rounds, Sandy began to feel that Barbados was the goal of his ambition.

Relaxing under the soothing influence of the alcohol that glided through his blood stream, Sandy took stock of his surroundings. The floor was crowded with tables seating two, three or four people of both sexes, all of whom were drinking and talking noisily. The air would have been thick if it hadn't been for the fact that a lovely sea breeze blew through from the verandah at the front facing the sea, right through to the dance floor beyond the saloon bar. It was on an extension Leo informed him, built out over a warehouse beneath but open to the tropic night. Dancing a paseo or a tango under a roof of stars Sandy felt, was a fitting setting for the fun and pleasure of getting a girl in your arms.

There was a small orchestra of violin, bass fiddle, piano, guitar and ukulele. The musicians, well primed by gifts of liquor, gave of their all. The dancing, naturally, was very spirited. The bar and dance floor obviously enjoyed the patronage of the sea-faring fraternity. Even the sea captains ventured to take the floor, and sweating blood, steered their unwilling charges through the uncharted seas of the dance floor exhibiting more in the line of seamanlike manœuvers than dancing skill. Through the racket, German, American, English and Scandinavian voices rose above the uproar from skippers, officers and engineers from all manner of ships, hell-bent on having as much fun as they could possibly squeeze out of their money and time ashore. To

Sandy's astonishment some Americans were flashing gold sovereigns, gold dollars and even gold dust about.

In answer to Sandy's query, Leo told him that they had got it constructing the Madera-Mamore railway in Brazil, usually at great cost to their health. Many were sick with tropical pellagra, beri-beri and worse diseases and were having a final fling before returning home for hospital treatment or, in some cases death.

'I don't see any 'little Englanders',' remarked Sandy.

'All respectable Bajans are in bed, sah, or just finishin wid de rubbers o' bridge at this time o' de night!' grinned Leo.

Every table had one or more female guests. The majority of them were white and some were coloured, but no black women. Leo informed Sandy that the Manager was very particular and 'didn't allow no black trash.' Leo certainly didn't consider himself as such. He was a man of means, a student of Codrington College and therefore one of the élite. He got up to dance an exaggerated tango with a mulatto named Kate from a neighbouring table who had attracted his attention. While he was thus energetically engaged, Sandy asked Jennie how come Leo got to Codrington College.

'Leo?' she laughed scornfully. 'Oh yeah! He was at Codrington College alright - he was the porter till he got fired for molestin' one o' the girls in the kitchen! Doan you go aroun' with that fella, Mistah Bank man, he no good! When you been here some time you find yo' own set all right. You're a nice boy! You watch yo'self!'

Sandy thanked her for the warning but privately thought Leo was doing a fine job of showing him Bajan night life. The sights Leo had to offer were just the kind he was interested to discover. The dance finished and Kate accompanied Leo back to the table where she stood four-square, hands on hips and glaring wickedly at the two white girls.

'What you white trash doin' heah?' she asked belligerently in a shrill voice. She was tall and thin with dark sallow skin and black eyes. Her floral silk frock was elegant if a trifle bizarre and her frizzy hair unruly despite the castor oil and bay rum with which it was liberally and pungently be-sprinkled. It stood out from her head and gave her an air of concentrated ferocity unbecomingly enhanced by a pair of venomously flashing eyes. Sandy fully expected the girls to quail before her but he had underestimated the Scottish strain. Jennie leisurely finished her drink.

'Kate,' she said calmly, 'If you wan' trouble, I'm ready for it and if you wan' dat black bastard, you're welcome to 'im, but please leave me alone when I'm entertainin' 'ristocratic company.'

'God dam' you, red leg!' spluttered Leo. 'You drink my money and call me bastud?'

Sandy told him soothingly that Jennie was talking drunk. He then appealed to the somewhat inattentive Sadie whose interest throughout was mostly taken with her drinks and trying to attract the attention of any male within reach.

'Doan worry boy,' she replied. 'Jennie'll fix dat Kate any time! She fixed her befo',' she added sagely.

Sensing serious trouble Sandy said hastily,

'Look here, why not let Kate join us. I'm a stranger here and I want to make as many friends as possible.' He tried to rise during this speech, but finding himself foundering a little, he subsided again, fervently hoping his diplomatic speech would pay off.

'Ok.' said Kate, a smirk replacing the scowl. 'I'll join you. No hard feelin's Jennie?'

'Ok by me,' replied Jennie, 'but lay off de Bank man, that's all!'

Kate sat down between Sandy and Leo, plonked her bony elbows on the table and promptly ordered a whisky sour.

'Jennie, if you like I'll fight you fo' de Bank man right now!' she said, giving Sandy an arch look.

'You'll do nothing of the sort!' he retorted. 'I don't want any woman. I just want to sit here and enjoy myself.'

'Cud deah! Maan, I do believe dis English boy is a cock-virgin!' squealed Kate in her high-pitched voice.

'Shut up!' Sandy said, anger sobering him. 'I'm going to dance!'

❧ Chapter 3 ❧

Sandy pushed back his chair determined to get to his feet at all costs and find any pretext to get away from the voracious Kate. With any luck perhaps she'd have gone by the time he got back, he thought hopefully. He opened his mouth to ask Jennie to join him in a tango but the words died on his open lips.

Through the smoke and haze, the most astonishingly beautiful young woman he had ever seen was moving gracefully towards him on the arm of a tall and extremely handsome young man. She passed the table without a glance. He could almost have said that she took his breath away.

She walked through the crowd without any awareness of anyone else being present. He watched her cross to a table given up to the two newcomers voluntarily by two coloured men, as if to Royalty. Her attention was given to the graceful act of seating herself under the care of her attentive escort. She looked up at the young man as he murmured something. Sandy fervently wished she would look at him instead. Unconsciously he smoothed his fair head as he took in the dark glossy locks of the man with her.

He sat down again and picked up his glass and took a reflective sip and caught a glassy-eyed look of awe riveted to Leo's face. He wasn't at all surprised and hoped he hadn't looked such a chump himself.

The couple were at a table only a little distance from theirs. Sandy was amply rewarded by a full view of the delectable girl. She couldn't be more than about eighteen or nineteen he surmised. She had the most striking features and unusual colouring. Her large eyes, to his fancy, were tiger-yellow. Her face was a perfect oval. She had a clear

28

golden complexion with russet colouring on the soft cheeks and a straight little nose above a full and passionate mouth. This was parted in a smile that showed off her pearly teeth as she answered the man with her. All this loveliness was framed by superb chestnut hair, which was caught up loosely with a deep yellow ribbon. As she turned to speak Sandy saw that it cascaded down her back in shining waves almost to her waist.

Fervently wishing the smile was for him, Sandy asked who she was.

'Maan, it's de Golden Girl - dat's Elmo!' Leo said in a voice sighing almost with reverence. He still looked as if he were in a trance.

Kate's eyes flashed across at the girl then back to her glass.

'She not so hot!' she muttered gratingly.

Jennie and Sadie however were gazing avidly at Elmo's gorgeous escort.

Sandy sipped his drink without taking his eyes off the glorious Elmo. Golden Girl! What a perfect description! She was wearing a white dress of some filmy material with puffed sleeves and a high waist that perfectly enhanced her lovely figure but added a look of sweet innocence to her youthfulness. She looked like a picture by Romney he thought. At the breast of this beautiful creature was a flower with petals of pale gold set in glossy leaves like the oleander and with what appeared to be some tiny green apples.

'What's the flower?' Sandy asked idly.

Leo's eyes fairly popped and the girls all exclaimed in unison.

'What's so odd?' enquired Sandy in surprise.

'Dat Elmo's mad - plain mad! Dat's Manchineel!' Leo cried in alarm. To Sandy's astonishment the word was whispered through the crowd almost from lip to lip and a hush fell as all eyes turned to the Golden Girl. Then the moment passed and the tide of noise rose once more.

'What's all this about Manchineel? Tell me,' said a bewildered Sandy, looking from one to the other.

'Boy,' said Leo. 'You see dat flower dat crazy girl wear? Dat's poison bush! Dem little green apples, if yo' eat 'em you go stark ravin' mad! Dat flower, if you pluck it, a sweet milky juice flow out and burn yo' skin like vitriol. You get dat juice on yo' head from standin' undah de tree, yo head swell up and yo' die ravin'! Nobody touch Manchineel, not in dis country. Nobody!' Leo's eyes rolled expressively in his head.

Kate shot a venomous glance in the direction of the beautiful girl. 'Dat Elmo Crofts is a big show-off! Mebbe some day she eat dem little green apples - I hope!'

'I think she crazy wearin' dat Manchineel,' remarked Jennie. 'It's bad luck. Anyway,' she shrugged, 'mebbe she just like dat flower. It's shu'is pretty. I used to pick it as a kid till I got burnt.'

'Yo' an' I been burnt a lot since, eh Jennie.' Kate laughed harshly.

'You've both been burnt?' queried Sandy innocently. Leo burst out laughing.

'In dis country, if yo' get burnt it mean you got some woo-man disease!'

Sandy attention was drawn inexorably to the other table, while his companions' gossip and bantering with each other washed over him unheeded. He was still entranced with Elmo's beauty.

He looked at the man with her. He certainly looked a fitting escort, immaculate and perfectly groomed, his black waving hair shining with hair oil. He was wearing what seemed to be some kind of military uniform in dark green. It had no regimental insignia however, but his bearing was that of a man of breeding and high rank. His fine eyes never left the face of the girl with him, but she seemed only interested in the bubbles rising in her champagne glass. Since she was no longer looking at her companion, Sandy thought he would will her to look up. If he could just catch her eye! But how to attract her attention and especially from such a good-looking and obviously wealthy admirer?

'Who's her friend?' he asked Leo.

'Some Venezuelan. Doan know what he doin' here, but he up to some funny business. A frien' told me he call on de Governor - yeah, de Governor at Government House, two, three, four times and every time de Governor say No! No! No! but Mr Ramon Corazon, he no elect to go away, he stay an' he say - 'Caramba, one day I see dat señor' and he say, Si! Si! Si! - He wait. No hurry.'

'What about Elmo? Who are her parents? Where does she live?'

'She live up de Bay road,' answered Kate, 'in a white bungalow wid green shutters. But it aint no use you callin' Bank man, she's crazy for this Corazon just now, so doan you waste yo' time on her! Anyway, she live wid Grand'ma de Lisle an' you doan want nothin' to do wid *dat* wicked ol' woo-man. She aint no Grandma tho', she really Elmo's aunt. Her brother was Elmo's ol' man. He was a widower some years an' when he died he left her to that worthless de Lisle woo-man.'

'Ladies and gents, I have an announcement to make!' said Sandy rising carefully to his feet. 'I shall now dance, and my partner will be the beauteous Elmo herself!'

'Mistah Mac,' cried Leo, 'please! My brudder make plenty trouble for me if I doan' bring you back safe an' soun'! This Venezuelan man carries a knife an' he stick yo' for sure if you take his woo-man!'

'Rot!' said Sandy. 'He's obviously a gentleman and will, I hope, recognise me as one, and gentlemen always understand one another.'

'Mistah Mac, you no savvy dis man's language. How can you tell him you be a gen'man?'

31

'Leo, you should know, if you were at Codrington College, that to recognise a gentleman, it is not necessary to know his language, but as it happens, I shall be able to address the señor in his own lingo!'

Letting go of the back of the chair he'd used as a support, he left an astonished Leo and the giggling girls and approached Elmo's table with an air of assurance and sangfroid.

'Permit me to introduce myself,' he said in Spanish. 'Señor Alexander MacNeil of the West Indian Bank.' The Venezuelan rose and shook the proffered hand. 'My name is Ramon Corazon, Señor and this is my friend Señorita Elmo Crofts.'

Sandy bowed to the girl with a smile. 'May I have the pleasure of this dance?'

'I perceive you are a caballero,' Corazon smiled pleasantly. 'I have no objection to Elmo dancing with you as I am an indifferent dancer.' And he handed the exquisite girl over to him.

As he took Elmo in his arms for the dance, Sandy felt his senses reeling and not from the alcohol either. Her soft resilient body swaying against him with the rhythm of the sensuous music, and the perfume of her hair - was it magnolia or frangipani - or even the deadly Manchineel at her delectable breast? - was the stuff of any young man's dreams. Her golden face with those parted lips gave him an overwhelming desire to kiss her. And that mouth cried out to be kissed! Through a tango, a pasé doblé and a waltz his senses swam at her closeness. She was an effortless dancer and her body responded to the music with great skill, but she made no attempt to engage with him. She had a serene confidence; a complete sureness of herself. She seemed absorbed more in their dancing, the rhythm and the music than him and made little attempt at conversation. Highly desirous of getting to know her, he asked her briefly about herself but she gave no satisfactory answer to his questions, just provoking looks from those tawny eyes, especially when he asked where he could find her again. As the waltz ended, she said,

'Let's get back to Ramon. I hate to leave him for long. He is so lonely.'

'Don't you like dancing with me?' he asked, disappointed and decidedly piqued.

'Of course I do. You dance very well and I love dancing, but I must be kind to Ramon.'

To hell with Ramon! he thought, but he took her back to the table with good enough grace, determined however to dislike this Corazon fellow heartily.

Ramon greeted her return with a loving smile and warm tenderness in his dark eyes. He then turned to Sandy.

'You will join us for a glass of wine Señor I hope? Please take a seat.' Motioning him to sit, he then fetched a champagne glass himself from a waiter and filled it to the brim, indeed till it was brimming over, from the bottle in the ice bucket beside him. He handed it to Sandy with a smile.

'Drink to the bright eyes of Elmo, Señor, and to my venture,' he said gaily as he took up his own glass. They bowed to Elmo and drank. As the Golden Girl put her glass to her lips she murmured fervently, 'To your venture Colonel Corazon!'

'Am I permitted to know what this venture is?' asked Sandy intrigued

'I regret,' he replied, 'that it is at present, sub rosa, - highly confidential, but this I can tell you, I am an outlaw in my own country, but the time is not far distant when I shall take my rightful place there.' He spoke quietly but with a passion that robbed the words of theatricality. All the same, Sandy thought he was slightly drunk.

After a few pleasantries while they finished off the champagne the Colonel lapsed into a moody silence. As he remained abstracted, Elmo and Sandy made flippant conversation. The several glasses of champagne seemed to have relaxed her. She became less conscious of her escort and Sandy was pleased to find that that she had a nice line in repartee. He felt he was perhaps making some little headway with her.

Their host roused himself.

'Señor MacNeil, we must leave you. Tomorrow, I have work to do. I must see the Governor of this island. I have important business with him; a question of armaments.' He smiled and rose, and wished their guest *Adios.*

'*Adios,* responded Sandy smiling, looking at Elmo as he got up.

Ramon offered his arm to Elmo. She spoke rapidly to him in an undertone and he turned to Sandy.

'Ring me one evening at the Beach Hotel. I am staying there and we will arrange another meeting if you should care for it.'

'I'd like that very much' Sandy replied thoroughly pleased, adding that yes, he would ring him without fail and thanked him, mentally registering the Beach Hotel as he had no idea where it was.

As the girl was swallowed up in the noisy crowd, Sandy found his interest in the place suddenly declining. The Scandinavian skippers were now at the stage of knocking the necks off their beers and drinking from the decapitated bottles. Kate and Jennie were hurling shrill imprecations at one another, the dancing had degenerated into the Bunny-hug and the sound of breaking glass and raucous voices were doing unpleasant things to the inside of his head. It was time to beat it.

Making his way a little unsteadily back to Leo's table he told them he was off.

'Home!' he repeated with finality.

'Good boy,' said Leo cheerfully. 'I recommne' dat. Fo' you first night out in Barbad's, you suah had a pow'ful good time Mistah Mac!'

Jennie and Kate forgot their argument. 'Mr Bank man, what come over you, you nevva dance wid us?' Jennie exclaimed aggrievedly, 'an' now you talk 'bout goin' home!'

'Dis man, he had de Obeah put on him by dat Manchineel,' sneered Kate. 'I reckon' he done fall fo' dat Elmo Crofts!'

'What's Obeah?'

'You no savvy Obeah, Bank man? Dat's black magic in dese parts. Black magic dat's all. Never been to Martinique or Haiti? Boy, dey call it Voo-doo dere. Never been to Africa? My gran' modder tell me it be Ju-ju over dere.'

'You put the wind up me with all this talk of black magic Kate. I'm off! *Adios amigos*' He waved a hand in farewell and then weaved his way to the door through the still-crowded tables. Leo's voice floated after him with vociferous instructions to rely on him for a bodyguard and guide, an-y time!

Since he knew the way and it wasn't far to his quarters Sandy felt he'd be quite safe by himself. He walked slowly along the quiet, deserted wharf-side by the Careenage, enchanted by the beauty of the tropical night. The coral wharf gleamed white in the vivid moonlight and the white schooners, strangely silent, swayed peacefully in the swell. The roofs of the warehouses caught the glorious moon glow. Sandy felt the tropics enter his soul.

It must have been gone three in the morning. Everyone asleep except the wanderer he thought, suddenly feeling uncannily alone. His thoughts went to the elusive Elmo again. He didn't want to think of her being with Ramon. Some vague hope that he could turn her thoughts from Ramon's dark charms to his own fair ones slipped into his mind. He knew he cut a good figure, but Ramon, he guessed had the distinct advantage of money, if not actual wealth. He chuckled at the thought of his lowly position as junior clerk in a bank. He stopped and listened to the water lapping against the piers and lifted his flushed face to the cool salt-laden breeze.

Refreshed but tired now, he strolled along to the now familiar iron gate leading to the rear of the bank. Upstairs no one stirred. In no time at all he was in his room, stripping off his clothes in the brightness of the moonlight that flooded through the window. Disregarding his scattered clothes, but with a moment's remorse for his suit flung negligently over his one chair, he edged carefully behind the mosquito net and slipped between the cool sheets with a contented sigh. He lay for a moment listening out for the tell-tale whine of a mosquito intruder that might have sneaked in with him. Silence. Lovely, he hadn't the energy to do battle with the bloody things tonight. Thinking of the beautiful Elmo, he drifted off to sleep.

❧ Chapter 4 ❧

The bright tropic sunlight streamed into the room from a cloudless blue sky as Theo, looking as glum as ever, approached the bed with a glass of fresh orange juice. But Sandy was already awake. Bridgetown as usual had been producing enough noise since the crack of dawn to awaken the dead.

'Mistah Mac' sah, time yo' was up. Seven o' clock an' yo' got to be in de Bank by eight. Have yo' barf an' I give yo a light breakfas' downstairs.'

The bath was in an outhouse in the courtyard and was fairly large and sunk into the ground. A plunge in its salt water did much to restore him after last night's binge and after a hasty breakfast, he joined his companions in the bank. Today was going to be starting the job in earnest.

The main doors were not yet open as business didn't commence till after nine. In the meantime, the Chief Cashier took Sandy, Leach and Joyner in hand and showed them their duties. For the time being, these would consist of 'posting' ledgers. This entailed entering cheques or monies in or drawn. This seemed simple enough and after meeting the rest of the staff, all Bajans, they were told to their surprise that they could now go and have breakfast.

This second breakfast was a fairly hefty meal taken in a restaurant outside the bank. Apparently, lunch was a light snack to be taken in the so-called lounge with the tattered hammock, but a late dinner was to be found at another and larger restaurant at a hotel out on the Savannah, a grassy park a couple of miles out of town. What Bank official devised this peripatetic mode of eating, Sandy never discovered but there was a certain satisfaction in it being quite out of the ordinary. Naturally this appealed to him;

anything that didn't smack of the humdrum was okay by him. He'd always had to overcome a certain impatience with ordinary life. It was possibly why he observed and took a genuine interest in anything, everybody and everything new as if to compensate for it. He felt a real need to enliven the more prosaic aspects of everyday life to make them tolerable.

Having got through a second breakfast, he went over to his allotted spot in the bank. Seated on a high stool at an old-fashioned sloping desk, he faced the biggest ledger he'd ever seen, stoutly bound in leather with enormous pages. A large pewter inkwell and an ordinary steel pen were his equipment. What, no quill pen? he thought. He regarded the vast ledger with some apprehension but he had no cheques to post as yet, so he had a look around.

The Bank, he mused, was certainly an agreeable place to work. The many doors and huge windows were all open, the ceilings very high and vaulted so that although outside the temperature was rising, the atmosphere within was thankfully cool and sheltered.

There were three tellers, each in his own large cubicle. The one directly in front of Sandy was to deal him his cheques and was an old and stooping man with a grey beard. To Sandy's youthful eyes he looked quite decrepit and he wondered at what speed the old man would work at and whether he'd have to bawl at him to get a move on. Sandy was much mistaken. He watched as the old man shovelled gold sovereigns out of a large sack that had been brought from the strong room, the gold cascading and tinkling musically from the copper shovel. Gold then was as common as copper. The British Empire had not yet had two wars to pay for. Sandy watched with fascination the old chap's quick effortless movements in weighing and counting the coins. As he discovered later, Pa, as he was known, was an expert with nimble fingers and an even nimbler brain.

Looking up from his massive ledger, Sandy noticed an elderly bald-headed clerk in a smaller cubicle peering at a list hanging up on the grille beside him. Intrigued, he hopped off his stool and went to have a closer look. The list was headed 'Rates of Exchange' and showed the value of the English pound in other currencies. Baldy looked at Sandy over his spectacles.

'You had better study that list in your spare time. You're the man that speaks umpteen languages. aren't you? Well, you won't be long on ledgers, you'll be on this counter and have ample opportunities for exercising your linguistic abilities on the foreign clients who come in here trying to pass dud money on you!'

'Great Scot!' Sandy said, 'and if they do pass dud money on me, who stands the racket?'

Baldy grinned and stroked his tobacco-stained moustache. 'You do my boy, you do! I've been on this counter for thirty years and I know every bank note in this hemisphere and they've even diddled me. Not often though,' he smiled wryly, 'not often!'

'Who decides on the rate of exchange?'

'Don't know my boy,' he said shrugging and going back to his work, 'unless it's the Twelve Elders of Zion, or Rothschild and his gold-plated brethren.'

After this cryptic answer Sandy returned to his ledger thinking perhaps he should have kept his mouth shut about his fluency in foreign languages.

Work in an English bank in those days was invariably at a leisurely pace. Not so at the Bridgetown branch of the West Indian Bank. It happened to be Market Day so business was brisk at first and later became a riot.

Sandy attempted posting cheques as they came along, until Pa, hearing the huge ledger leaves flailing back and forth in Sandy's anxiety to keep up with the number of ever-increasing entries, came over to his side. He suggested that he wait and collect a good fistful of cheques and paying-in slips, put them in alphabetical order and then start posting. 'In this way,' Pa said, 'you'll only have two or three postings for the entire day instead of dozens.'

Grateful for this advice and being a quick worker, Sandy soon got along at speed. Naturally this needed his close attention so he found little time to examine the crowd in front of Pa's grille or the stream of motley clients at Baldy's counter all of whom with his innate curiosity he was longing to study.

Very soon he felt he *had* to get to his feet to deal with that immense ledger and the continuous flow of slips and cheques. He found however, he really did need the stool to get to grips with it efficiently. It took him a while to find the right mode of attack.

As noon approached and the press of people increased and with the sun nearing its zenith, it was hot even in the bank. He noticed that in the best English tradition the established Bank officials strictly adhered to the belief that shirt sleeves were undignified. Fully suited, they worked on with unruffled calm and no appearance of perspiring at all. Pa in his black alpaca jacket looked for all the world as if he were in Threadneedle St; cool and unflurried, his pen flying over the paper or his nimble fingers snapping the dollar notes, swiftly counting coins, or dipping his shovel into his sack to weigh the larger amounts in his gleaming balance with complete sangfroid.

As the heat increased, Sandy however, had to slip out of the jacket of his white drill suit and work in his shirt sleeves. Heavens, this is the tropics alright, he thought.

Lunch was in relays and for Sandy consisted of fruit and a Pimms No. 1. The older members ate at their desks among the inkwells, others gravitated upstairs. One of the clerks, a big Bajan of about 40 ate the strangest lunch; two hard boiled eggs washed down with a large brandy watered down by a bottle of Belfast ginger ale. Sandy never ever saw him vary it and it didn't seem to do him any harm either!

Barbados currency was going to take some getting used to he found. It was the strangest on record. It used the decimal system speaking in dollars and cents and had paper five and ten dollar notes on the West Indian Bank. The coin however, was in gold and silver and English. Very confusing, but the decimal he found, was much easier to calculate than shillings and pence.

After lunch he was called over to watch a letter being duplicated on a pre-historic thing called a Cyclostyle. He was told he'd need to learn to use the thing so pay attention.

This oddity really caught his interest. He'd never seen anything like it. It was a lead tray about an inch deep filled with pressed, smoothed wet clay. The document was written out in thick black ink in an antique mode called 'bordereau' he was carefully informed. Then it was laid face down on the wet clay. A rubber roller was passed over it to transfer the ink. Copies were taken until the ink was exhausted, which didn't alas take long. Still, it was better than nothing he thought wryly.

He soon discovered that the Bank had no adding machines. He was told that it was up to him to add up his ledger for himself. It certainly didn't bother him as he was good with figures. Fiscal ability ran in his Scots blood.

Looking around he also noticed that everything was being written by hand. There was no sign at all of a typewriter. It all seemed so incredibly old-fashioned. It wasn't long before Sandy found that the old chaps were equally skilled in hand writing everything. They were fast and flawless and there seemed no appreciable delay at all.

There was one innovation though. A telephone. But it must have been one of the first Sandy thought, eyeing the long wooden thing with a handle one wound to summon the exchange. Yet he readily admitted later that despite the lack of modern aids the Bank seemed efficient to a very high degree.

At last, 3 o' clock came when all good Banks, at least in the British Empire, closed for the day.

'Now then you chaps,' said the Chief Cashier to the three newcomers, 'finish your posting, strike a balance and you can push off.'

Suits me, thought Sandy and concentrated so well on the job that he was the first to finish. If there was pleasure or leisure in the offing Sandy could work more surely and quickly than anyone. It was one of his strongest characteristics. There was little use waiting for his stick-in-the-mud colleagues, Leach and Joyner, who in all probability would be off to have afternoon tea or write letters home, so changing into flannels and providing himself with a towel, he went shopping.

He had three essential purchases to make. The first and most pressing was a pair of dark glasses. The sun reflected off the thick white coral dust of the roads as from sheets of glass. The glare was blinding, especially when coming out of the comparative dimness of the Bank.

The next was a bicycle. But a bike was necessary unless one wanted to ride in the noisy and hopelessly dusty mule-driven trams. Also, there was so much he wanted to explore that he couldn't do on foot. He soon found one but at the extortionate price of £10.

The last was a swim-suit. The glorious warm waters round the island were perfect for swimming, but Leo had already warned him of the sharks and the nasty snapping habits of a big evil fish known as the barracouta. This monster had a great tendency to snap at objects dangling in the water and since it was the fashion to swim naked, many a native Bajan had been involuntarily castrated by the beast's sharp teeth. Sandy had no intention of giving the barracouta any such chance, tempting though swimming naked seemed.

Grateful for the glasses, and with the new swimsuit tucked into the towel and fixed to the back of the bike, Sandy mounted it and in tearing high spirits set off over Chamberlain Bridge and along the Bay road towards Hastings. He'd been told this was the best place near the town for batheing.

The heat of the day was passing and a fresh sea breeze had sprung up and cooled his skin refreshingly as he pedalled along. He passed quite mediocre buildings; some stuccoed, some stone, alternating with wooden shacks. Bridgetown could not be famed for its architectural beauty, that's for sure, he thought. He cycled passed a poor Negro quarter and then some prosperous bungalows and soon covered the two miles to Hastings.

It had a short but obviously unfinished promenade with a bandstand at the end. He wondered idly what had made the money run out. There was also a little pier jutting out to sea and acres of fine coral sand and the clearest water he'd ever seen. It looked wonderfully inviting.

He stripped off and changed in a bathing box and plunged into the warm water, well away from the shadows cast by the pier where the ugly barracouta was prone to lurk. He revelled in the silky warmth of the water, so different from the chilly though invigorating seas that he was more familiar with off his native Aberdeen in far off Scotland.

He swam out a considerable distance and found he could still see the bottom. Swimming right down under water he could clearly see the blood red coral reef, crowded with multi-coloured sea anemones and sea plants.

A wonderful variety of vivid fish of every colour, size and shape swam around him with great unconcern. Their acceptance of his presence he found extraordinary and charming. Some darted in little shoals, some poked around in solitary splendour amongst the coral growth. Others were quite startling and one had fins as large as a bird's wing but like gossamer. He noticed all sorts of sea creatures, some of which he could only vaguely identify, going about their business on the sea floor although some of these scuttled for safety immediately they sensed his presence. Everywhere he looked there was movement and colour and novelty. How could anyone be bored in this bright tropic world he wondered?

As he came out of the water, he felt there was one thing and only one thing needed to complete this tropical idyll - a beautiful girl. Ah! Elmo, he sighed! She was certainly fitted for this exotic place. Alas she had the handsome Ramon. Well, there's nothing else for it, I'll have to find someone else, he thought, drying himself off in the still warm air. As he got dressed however, he began to think of his dinner.

Dusk fell swiftly, and suddenly it was night. The promenade, short though it was, was obviously the popular place to enjoy the night air. It was filling up with people, laughing talking or milling about and they were soon accompanied by an enthusiastic band. Dancing started almost as they struck up. A lively night life was already well under way. Very hungry by this time, Sandy left them to it and went off on his bike for his evening meal and the delights of Bridgetown.

❧ *Chapter 5* ❧

The regular place for the evening meal was the Stafford Hotel out at a grassy park called the savannah, a mile or so out of town. Sandy enjoyed sitting at one of the small tables in the evening and looking out over the moon- or star-lit savannah through the pillared porticoes of the ground floor. Open to the evening breezes and with a wide pavement with people passing by to look at too, it was a popular watering hole. It had its share of residents as well as a passing population and was a regular meeting as well as eating place.

Leach and Joyner were eating with him one evening, when the fourth chair at the table was pulled out and boisterously taken by a very odd-looking character. It was Dunster, a journalist from one of the local papers. He was nicknamed Thunder and Lightning; whether from his journalism or the speed of his comings and goings was a matter for conjecture.

'Well fellas, what's the news?' he asked in his deep booming voice, his dark eyes glistening in the extreme pallor of his face.

'You ought to be able to tell us that,' said Joyner, 'that's your trade.'

'Hey,' said Thunder, 'I don't mean that kind of news, I mean any new girls! You know my hobby!' He ran a hand over the few hairs remaining on his head, his face glistening with dewy perspiration and chuckled gleefully. He looked like a pale satyr. He was only in his mid-twenties and his dinner jacket suit, which hung untidily on his gaunt frame, badly needed brushing. His tie was frayed and poorly tied.

While he waited for his soup course, he ordered a large whisky and soda. As soon as it arrived, he seized it and drank it thirstily in gulps. Just then a lightly coloured native girl in a red frock with a hibiscus bloom in her glossy black hair dawdled by outside on the pavement. Dunster seemed galvanised. His black eyes flashed and he jumped up, rocking the table.

'Don't wait for me lads! I'll be back for the next course!' and out he shot in the direction of the disappearing girl. It was a moonless night so he was lost to sight almost at once.

'Great Scot! What an eccentric cove! I never heard of anyone chasing a girl in the middle of his dinner before!' exclaimed Sandy.

'You don't know Dunster,' said Leach morosely. 'The sight of a skirt would make him leave his mother's funeral. Don't worry, he'll be back for the next course alright.'

'Oh?' said Sandy. 'How come you know all about our eccentric news hound Leach?'

Leach scowled. 'Oh, I know about him alright. A few weeks ago, I was standing with my bike, talking to Rodriguez the Mexican when Dunster joined us. He just floated out of the dark as if from nowhere the way he usually does and was puffing away at one of those awful Brazilian cigarettes. What a stink! Anyway, the Mex was telling me about a pretty Brazilian girl who had taken a room over Maxie's bar on the Hastings road. She had just come up from Manàos - have you heard of it? It's a thousand miles up the Amazon. Very few if any women ever come back out of it apparently.' he said.

'Leach,' smiled Sandy wickedly, 'you seem remarkably well-informed on a side of life in which I thought you had very little interest.'

'The interest was forced on me,' bristled Leach, 'Rodriguez is one of the Bank's clients, that's how I know the man.'

'Carry on,' said Sandy.

'It appears,' continued Leach in his usual peevish tone, 'that the young woman was abandoned by some American skipper who had tired of her and said he was beating it back to his native Seattle. Rodrigez then remarks that she is a lovely woman and only working to get her fare back to Manàos. Damnable Dunster then seizes my bike!

'Leach old man, just let me have your bike for ten minutes!' and before I could say a word, he had mounted it and was pedalling off at high speed! The Mexican thought it very funny and said, 'Ah that Mister Dunster, he work fast, too fast!'

'Sounds perfectly feasible to me!' said Sandy.

Leach smiled sourly. 'That's not all! Thunder and Lightning, true to his rotten name, tore off, and apparently, instead of dismounting outside Maxie's in a normal manner, rang a violent peal on the damn bicycle bell and rode hell for leather into the bar and crashed into the counter taking a headlong dive over it, - bottles, glasses and God knows what shooting everywhere, - leaving my bike to crash to the floor! I heard the whole episode from Maxie later.'

A disgruntled Leach then went on to tell how Dunster had dashed up the stairway at the back regardless of Maxie's shouts and curses at all the damage. Maxie had charged up after him to the landing with the intention of throwing Dunster out whereupon the Brazilian lady appeared at the door of her room, considerably frightened at seeing Dunster looking like a wild man, who then, - all sweetness and light, bowed low over her hand and murmured over it in fluent Portuguese. The girl was so charmed by his excellent manners that she then admitted him without more ado and shut the door in the outraged Maxie's face.

Leach, much put out by Sandy's obvious enjoyment, pursed up his mouth, his face the picture of disapproval.

'A man of engaging address it seems, and one who will brook no delay when on amour bent!' Sandy laughed. 'But did he remember to return the bike?'

'He came back with the bike alright, but it wasn't just ten minutes, more like half an hour. The front mudguard was bent all to hell and the lamp was skew-wiff. He apologised of course and said he'd pay for the damage,' Leach said grudgingly.

Sandy laughed and said with some admiration, 'Strikes me as a kind of Elizabethan!'

'Funny you should say that!' interjected Joyner, 'he does think he's an Elizabethan. It's an obsession with him. He wants to grow a beard from the period of all things, but said he couldn't stick it in this heat. With beards still the fashion at home, perhaps he'll go back there and try it out - with any luck,' Joyner sniggered.

'Can't see him leaving the erotic delights of the tropics just for that,' rejoined Sandy, amused at the mental image of Dunster's sparse locks offset by a pointed beard of all things. 'Wonder if he carries a poignard in his sock like the Scots skhian dhuh.'

Leach and Joyner looked blank so Sandy ignored them.

The meal had passed the fish course and the meat was being served when Dunster appeared, true to his promise. He looked as if he'd gone through quite an ordeal in the short time he'd been away. The knees of his evening trousers were wet and muddy, his collar was limp and his hands trembled. He called for a large whisky.

'You seem to have enjoyed yourself,' said Sandy with mild sarcasm.

'It's alright at the time,' he said looking sheepish, 'it's the aftermath! - Confound it!' he burst out. 'I forgot I had to see Ines tonight and now I'm not able to do her justice!'

'Who's Ines?' queried Sandy.

'Oh, a Brazilian I know. She lives over Maxie's bar. Would you like to visit her for me and tell her I'm having a crisis of nerves? I can recommend Ines, she is so nicely maternal, no rough stuff if you know what I mean. Not like these half-castes, they nearly kill a man!'

48

Sandy declined the honour of calling on Ines, but Leach readily agreed to carry Thunder's message to the guest over Maxie's Bar. Leach avoided his eye as Sandy looked sardonically at him.

'Are you sure it's only a message you're carrying to Ines?' Sandy asked, diverted by the thought of the priggish Leach frequenting a dive like Maxie's.

Leach flushed.

Having discovered the joys of swimming within such easy distance of the Bank, Sandy got into a daily habit of refreshing himself at Hastings' beach after his day's labours.

One afternoon as he was warming himself on the sands after a swim, he noticed two good-looking women in swim-suits leaving a bungalow by a short stairway to the sands. They turned along the beach in his direction. They were both singularly attractive with perfect figures and long legs.

Admiring their graceful advance, Sandy thought he'd like nothing better than to get acquainted. As they approached, he saw that the taller of the two was older and appeared to be about 40, while the other was only about 18. Their immaculate swimsuits were moulded to their slim bodies and looked very fashionable to his eye, always conscious of women's looks and grooming. Both of them had their dark hair done in a very long braid to one side.

He soon realised that they were not white as he'd first thought, but nearly white. With their lightly tanned skin, glossy dark hair and brown eyes they were very alluring and Sandy was eager to talk to them.

As they got nearer, he got up and made some fatuous remark about the water being fine. They paused and the older woman smiled and to Sandy's astonishment answered in a cultured English voice, 'When you are dressed, please walk into my house and make yourself at home until we have had our swim. We won't be long. If you'd care for a drink, just ring and the girl will bring you one.'

With a gracious smile showing beautiful white teeth, she walked down to the water's edge followed by the young girl who also smiled engagingly at him.

Somewhat taken aback but charmed by such kind hospitality, he sat awhile on the sand and watched them swimming with elegant ease in the warm turquoise sea. When he was dry, he dressed and headed down the beach to their bungalow. Mounting the short flight of steps, he entered the house, delighted at such an unlooked-for invitation and blessing his good fortune in meeting such personable women.

What a contrast to his dingy Bank quarters! The floors shone. Rugs of wild animal skins and brightly-coloured woven mats were scattered attractively over the polished wood. The furniture was rosewood and walnut and silver gleamed on a massive sideboard. Richly patterned cushions lay on brocaded settees and Berbice chairs. The jalousies, venetian-type shutters, were half-closed giving the room an invitingly shady coolness that was soothing after the glare from the coral sands. A fragrance filled the air, perhaps from the profusion of flowers in the house or maybe it was a combination of the perfume of women and rich furnishings.

With a sigh of pure delight, Sandy sank into a comfortable Berbice chair and banged a bell on a side table. Instantly a stout and very black maid appeared.

'Mistah, nobody at home!'

'I know,' answered Sandy. 'I've just met the lady of the house on the beach. She asked me to sit and wait for her here.'

'Very good, Sah. I tink mebbe you like a flip if yo' just been in de water,' she replied, surprising Sandy by taking him completely at his face value and unquestioningly ready to extend that hospitality that seemed to abound in the tropics.

He hadn't any idea what a flip was, but waited expectantly and in a very short while the maid returned with a glass filled with what turned out to be a delicious concoction of iced milk, eggs and brandy, well and truly swizzled. She also handed him a box of Brazilian cigarettes and a light, then left him to enjoy his drink and smoke.

Delighted by the elegance around him, he was nonetheless a little puzzled at the comfort of his surroundings. He had the idea that people with even the faintest hint of coloured blood in their veins belonged to the submerged tenth, relegated to the second rate or worse, but here were two obviously coloured women living in luxury and artistic comfort. Who and what were they?

As he luxuriated and sipped his drink, he heard the rustle of beaded curtains behind him. He sprang up to see two perfectly groomed women in European evening dress enter the room and come smiling towards him. They were his acquaintances from the beach. The elder held out her hand to him.

'Let me introduce myself, Aimée Danse and this is my niece, Lois.'

'My name's Alexander MacNeil. I'm with the local Bank.' He bowed slightly and shook the proffered hand, liking its cool firm clasp. 'Delighted to meet you.'

'Please sit down, Mr MacNeil. I hope you have been comfortable while you have been waiting?'

'Oh, I have, thank you.'

The maid entered with drinks for the women, a flip for Lois and a clear drink for Aimée.

'Is this your first visit to the West Indies?'

'Yes,' Sandy admitted, 'and the first time I've been so far away from home. I haven't actually been here very long.'

'We thought so. We have seen you several times on the beach and thought you must be new here. You are most welcome here in our house. We will be very happy for you to visit if you care for it,' she smiled.

'I'd like that very much,' said Sandy with unfeigned pleasure.

'While you are finding your feet, we shall be glad to be your friends and help fill in some of your spare time. But,' she added, 'I'm afraid that for your sake it will have to be quite sub rosa.'

'You mean I shall have to see you on the quiet? But why, for goodness' sake?'

Aimée smiled reassuringly but her fine eyes were rueful. 'Social distinctions are very strong on this Island,' she answered, 'so really it is my duty to warn you about it. We believe it is very much to do with a guilty conscience on the part of the whites. You see, their morals have left a lot to be desired. You can see that very much evidenced in the streets of the town, yes, even in their own homes. I don't suppose,' she continued, 'that there is any other part of the world where there is such an inter-mixture of black and white blood. Lois and I are coloured, and therefore in more senses than one, quite 'beyond the pale.' We are consequently not included in white social life. You will find sooner or later my dear Mr MacNeil that you will be called severely to task if your white friends find you have been hob-nobbing with Lois and myself,' she finished with a regretful smile.

'I can't believe it!' Sandy burst out incredulously. 'You are obviously educated and cultured people, if I might say so! There are plenty people I've met, even over here, who couldn't hold a candle to you! I don't understand it at all,' he said, feeling that this was such awful bosh. 'This is all very sad,' he added.

Looking at Lois, she seemed not in the least put out. He wasn't sure whether to take Aimée seriously or not.

'Pay no attention to Lois,' said Aimée. 'She treats the whole thing as a joke! She's spent half her life in England so she cannot appreciate the seriousness as I do. I have lived here longer and find it harder to live down my colour.'

Aimée changed the subject and they talked comfortably of other things. Presently Sandy got up to go and was accompanied to the door by the two women who both caused his pulse to flutter as they rested their delicate hands on his arms. He marvelled anew at having spent a lovely afternoon with two such elegant and glamorous women.

The maid came forward and pointed out his bike leaning at the foot of the stoop. 'Ah found yo' bike sah, by de bathing machines and brought it heah fo' safety.' with that she vanished into the house.

'Sadie is a good girl,' said Aimée. 'I've an idea,' she continued with a somewhat grim smile, 'that she is distantly related to me.'

'Listen,' said Sandy as he shook hands, 'I should very much like to see you again soon.'

'That would be delightful,' said Aimée. 'Slip up one night after dark so that you won't be observed and we'll give you a typical Barbadian meal and welcome. Hopefully we can be friends and you can have some evenings with us until you find your feet. You will soon have shoals of invitations later to more formal and proper dinners with the society element and then you won't care to associate with us again.' She added this without rancour, but just a trace of regret in her voice.

'Don't you believe it!' he said stoutly. 'You are my first friends and I intend that you shall remain so!'

'What a lovely thought!' giggled Lois. 'Hope you don't change your mind!'

'Of course I won't,' he said with smiling conviction.

Making his adieux, he made off down the darkening road to Bridgetown, congratulating himself on his good luck. Very soon the night, as always, came down like a knife. Before long he found that despite the white coral of the road still showing up like a ribbon before him, he had to dismount and kindle his bike's oil lamp. As he did so he noticed a trim white bungalow by the roadside with jalousies that showed bright green in his lamp. A white verandah surrounded the front porch and one or two magnolias by the house shed their delicate fragrance into the night.

I wonder if this is Elmo's house, he mused, the one Kate talked about, on the Bay road. He hesitated but there was no sign of life, no lights, the place seemed deserted.

Remounting his bike, he rapidly increased his pace. The hard coral surface was ideal for cycling and he made good speed, meeting only the occasional buggy, cyclist or strolling native on the way. He had to return to his rooms to bath and change and then retrace part of his route to Stafford House where he was to dine, but this double journey was getting to be a pattern of his life since he was forever out and about. Partly to avoid the depressing Bank quarters, but also to pursue as much fun as possible with the exuberance of youth that he had in abundance. The golden days and balmy tropic nights were always beckoning a young man brought up to the rigours of the cold and Scots Presbyterianism that were his native country.

❦ *Chapter 6* ❦

One evening a few weeks later Sandy found Dunster the reporter, or newspaper-man as he preferred to be known, sitting alone at a table at Stafford House. This table was nearest the Savannah so that he could keep a weather eye out for any ships or prostitutes that might pass in the night.

'Have a scotch' he hailed Sandy. 'I've only had two and a pink gin.'

'Don't mind a rum swizzle if there's one going. Where are my two pals from the Bank?'

'Deserted you, or rather me, in favour of far more respectable company,' and he indicated another table occupied as usual by a resident at the hotel, a bible vendor from British Guiana.

'Just so,' returned Sandy as he sat down casting his eye about the room at the two dozen or so tables. 'Well, I don't mind at all. I see enough of those two birds in the daytime. Furthermore,' he added pleasantly, 'we'll be freer to discuss beer, rum, sociology and the shadier side of your life, my dear Thunder.'

'God they're a dreary lot,' said Dunster morosely following Sandy's glance and roaming over their other dining companions.

'Just the usual motley crowd you'd find at any boarding house or hotel in England I'd say.'

'Hmm!' grunted Dunster signalling a waiter again. 'Not exactly fodder for my newspaper old boy. And no doubt leading blameless lives of stultifying boredom by the look of 'em. No decent conversation.'

'What? Not even old Professor Goops? He's an interesting old cove.' Sandy had got into conversation with him and his charming English wife on a couple of evenings.

They were also residents at the Stafford. The professor's real name was Teufelmann, but his students at Oxford had christened him with the Greek name for his supposed resemblance to a vulture. A somewhat overweight one, Sandy thought but greatly appreciated the wit of this allusion and agreed. Goops did have a rather predatory face, with hooded eyes which were slightly protuberant and invariably blood-shot. The skin of his neck was red and leathery but was probably more the fault of the tropics, Sandy decided. He was a Prussian German, an anthropologist from Columbia University and an avowed atheist. Although he was extremely well-informed and intensely engrossing Sandy found, religion was obviously his pet subject. Steering him onto other subjects was hard going as Goops kept looking for openings to get back on his hobby-horse.

'Frightful old bore,' Dunster replied. 'Did he try to palm one of his tracts off on you? No? Give the old sod time! He's done his own translation of the 17th Century anti-Catholic writings of the vituperative Dupuis, although Goops' wife's a devout Catholic. He can't wait for everyone to share his foul views. Trust old Goops to choose to translate someone who had the honour to be on the Church's *Index Expurgatorius.* Paid for it himself too. It hasn't entered his fat Prussian head however, that religion is one of the things educated Englishman simply will not argue about. He's always putting peoples' backs up.'

'Thanks for the tip, I must remember not to mention Voltaire!' replied Sandy with a grin.

His drink arrived and he sampled it and settled back to await the food.

'I met a woman here the other day who might have amused you old chap. Not for your particular proclivities, mind Dunst. She was American, an antique dealer of all things, busy over here denuding the West Indies of their valuable old furniture and jewellery. I asked her if stripping the place of all these charming assets was quite the thing, but she said that judging by the number of American cars she had seen on the Islands, they were getting a fair return.'

'Those American cars,' boomed Dunster with a cynical smile, 'are stolen on the streets of New York, repainted and then shipped over here to dealers in the Caribbeas!'

'I like your jaded view of life Thunder old chap,' said Sandy wryly giving him a mock toast.

'True! Every word.'

Meanwhile, Sandy's Bank colleagues were sitting looking very genteel in hard collars, stiff shirts and black dinner jackets, their heads glossy with Honey and Flowers hair oil, bending an attentive ear to the bible salesman.

'Your pals don't like me, 'complained Dunster. 'They told our revered hostess dear old Miss Weir, that I wasn't quite the thing, my behaviour was execrable and they were sure their parents wouldn't care for them to associate with a fellow like me. Also, they might get a bad name in Barbados and they do want to meet the right people!'

'Never mind Thunder, I won't desert you. I have a taste for low characters like yourself. Let's have another drink.'

'Good idea. It'll wash down the taste of the grub. And keep away from 'dem coloured folk' Jock, you'll regret it!' warned Thunder using what he thought was a suitable Scotch appellation for Sandy. 'Look what they've done to me? I would sooner you made a pal of Mr Meek.'

'Who's Mr Meek?'

'Mr Meek is your pals' respectable friend, the Agent for the Foreign Bible Vendors Incorporated and indeed his is a very sad case,' replied Dunster in his most lugubrious manner, 'a very sad case. But alas, I can't print it.'

Sandy knew that when Dunster put on that fiddle face he was getting humorously tight. He'd already drunk several large whiskies and God knows how many cocktails before that.

'Come on then, let's have your story, but leave the scotch and get on with your boiled mutton.'

Dunster looked distastefully at the food on his plate. 'I hate boiled mutton, in fact I hate mutton in any shape, except the one you know,' he added with a leer.

'Cut the vulgarity and tell me about Mr Meek and his very sad case.'

'Well,' said Dunster looking like the grave-digger in Hamlet, 'it is a case of 'wice over wirtue' as Sam Weller would have said. Not many moons ago, Mr Meek held a position of some note in Alexandria. He was reckoned to be the most successful Bible salesman in Egypt. But, alas for fame. His star was due for an eclipse. The Foreign Bible Vendors Inc employed a newcomer to join Mr Meek in bible vending. An Armenian Jewish gentleman who told Mr Meek he had been converted to the true faith, had seen the light, had testified and so on. To my jaded mind, it has a decidedly humorous turn.'

Sandy looked sardonic and continued eating. Dunster chuckled and took a gulp from his glass again. He forked some of the mutton into his mouth, chewed grimly, swallowed and resumed.

'Anyway, all went well in the bible stakes. The Armenian gentleman who rejoiced in the name of Stenkah, made good; he made very good. He proved to be a go-getter, a super-vendor of bibles! In fact, he sold bibles to the most unlikely people, to Pharisees and publicans alike! To Australian sailors, to soldiers, Turks, Syrians, Levantines, anybody! All would stop and buy one from Stenkah and pay gladly for it!' Dunster, eyes gleaming, looked more lugubriously than ever. 'Mr Meek's stock went down badly. He became an also-ran and the F.B.V. Inc. who used to be so pleased with him signified their intention of promoting Mr Stenkah over his head if he didn't buck his ideas up!' Thunder was in full flood now. revelling in his story-telling.

'Mr Meek became very depressed. He had a wife and six children dependant on him. He admired Mr Stenkah's salesmanship and approved of the manner in which he was disseminating the word. He thought of applying for a transfer to some part, perhaps at less salary and commission so that he would not have to compete with this superman…'

Once more Dunster refreshed himself and emptying his glass, ordered a fresh drink from the waiter arriving with more food while Sandy looked at him with huge enjoyment. There was no stopping Thunder now.

'But,' he continued, waggling a pale hand, as if lost without a glass in it, 'there was one fine day, when Stenkah rushed into the store for more bibles where Mr Meek was sadly contemplating his stock of unsold wares. Stenkah kept his own stock securely locked in a cupboard which he quickly unlocked, and seizing an armful, he tore out at his usual speed as if Salvation just couldn't wait, but in his hurry, he dropped a bible which fell at Mr Meek's feet. Old Meek was interested to see two objects fall out of the sacred volume. He picked them up; one was a card, a sort of large visiting card and the other a small sealed envelope. Meek regarded these two curiously. The card, in nice copperplate writing informed the reader that the 'Ould Nails' was nothing compared to the establishment of Mrs Judgapreeks, whose address was obligingly given with a tiny map to show the exact location. Mr Meek trembled and when he opened the small envelope, he found to his horror that it contained a white powder. Old Meek hadn't lived all those years in Egypt for nothing. He identified both articles at once. Cocaine and the address of a brothel. These were the reasons for Mr Stenkah's rising sales! And enclosed in each copy of the sacred book no less! He was horrified and his mind was in a whirl. Should he go to Russell pasha, the terror of the drug vendors, who would speedily put the manacles on Stenkha? But no, the F.B.V. Inc should be instantly apprised of the methods of this snake-in-the-grass, so taking pen and paper our good Mr Meek sat down then and there and wrote to the Managing Director in Cairo telling him the facts and enclosing the incriminating evidence in a registered envelope.'

'Good Lord! Was Stenkah arrested?'

'Don't be silly,' said Dunster. 'he was promoted. Meek was fired. The F.V.B. Inc. didn't believe Mr Meek, said he'd invented the whole thing out of jealousy for Stenkah's success and promoted the super salesman Head Bible Vendor, but in view of Meek's long service he was not actually fired but translated to British Guiana where he would have time to reflect on his conduct and sell bibles to the ignorant heathen on the sugar estates of the Colony.'

'You're pulling my leg, Dunst!' said Sandy laughing incredulously.

'Am I? Then ask old Meek yourself. I daresay he's regaling your pals with the frightful injustice of things in this naughty world. And talking of brothels,' Thunder continued, 'Let's go up to Elmo's after you've finished guzzling that awful plate of sapodillas.'

Sandy was annoyed. 'Are you talking of Elmo Crofts?'

'Sure,' said Dunster. 'You seem peeved. Have you met her?'

'Yes once. I'm crazy about her. She's beautiful!'

'Don't be an ass. She's a good-looker alright but she has no virtue, not since her grandmother sold her to the American drummer. You know, travelling salesman, or in English, commercial traveller.'

'What do you mean, *sold* her?'

'Well practically. Don't look so astonished. You're away from home now laddie and in the wild and woolly tropica, I mean the exotic and erotic tropics. Have you noticed a nice trim little white bungalow with green jalousies not far from Hastings?'

Sandy nodded tersely, eyes smouldering.

'Well, that's where Elmo and her old hag of a grandmother hang out. You walk on to the verandah. Elmo comes out. Unknown to you, you are weighed up by the old hag through a hole in the partition and she bellows, 'Five dollars!' or 'Ten dollars!' according to your age and look of affluence. Elmo then invites you into the parlour for a drink but you never see the old hag. She disappears. Ugly as sin probably.'

'Dunster, this is murder! How long has this been going on?' asked Sandy, stunned.

'Six months, maybe a year.'

'But she may have V.D. for all we know!'

'Not much fear of that, the old grandma's too fly for that and probably has Elmo well-warned and instructed. No Bajans or coloured folk are admitted. She specializes in strangers who look as if they can pay. Personally, I'm not one of the elect, but I keep on trying.'

Briefly relieved that this mad lecherous character at least hadn't had his hands on the exquisite girl, Sandy exclaimed heatedly, 'I've never heard of anything so disgusting and cruel! What a waste of a beautiful creature! The old hag's not really her grandmother, is she?'

'No, her name's Leila de Lisle and she hails originally from Haiti, a sister of Elmo's mother, so she's her aunt. Both the girl's parents are dead, but the father left a fair sum of money to de Lisle who was eventually found in Buenos Aires, on the condition she cared for the kid. It's my belief the old hag is a woman of easy virtue getting on in years and probably latterly head bummer in a knocking shop in Buenos Aires. Anyway, the de Lisle bought the white bungalow from a French tart who was working her passage home by degrees from Rio, bought furniture et al and set Elmo and herself up in business as it were.'

'But what,' Sandy said indignantly, 'is the law doing about it? Can nobody save this beautiful child?'

'You sound like the Salvation Army Jock! Does Elmo want to be saved? I doubt if you could prove anything and who is to give evidence? I haven't heard of any complaints except those whose custom has been turned down, - and one of those is a member of the Legislative Council and he like me, still lives in hopes!'

'You should all be shot!' raged Sandy, cut to the heart at this horrible news. 'Perhaps I'll save her myself!'

'Go ahead Jock, go ahead! But mind the old hag doesn't knife you!'

'Come on then!' he said. 'Let's go up and see the girl!'

Sandy jumped up and headed off towards Miss Weir's shed where they kept their bikes with Dunster lumbering behind. They both made off up the road to Hastings.

Despite his inner turmoil, Sandy could not help enjoying cycling along the deserted road in the bright moonlight with no street lamps to disturb its radiance, the fragrance of tropical flowers assailing his nostrils and glimpses of the sea at intervals along the way. Only the rustling of the leaves in the palm trees and the occasional sound of a guitar or Negro voice disturbed the warm, tranquil night. A cool breeze agreeably fluttered their thin clothing.

'How do you know all of this anyway Thunder?' he asked hoping that Dunster had got it all wrong. He wouldn't put it past him to have made it up.

'I'm a newspaperman old boy, I hear everything. Anyway, I met Elmo's first customer, the American who started her decline from virtue, so I had what happened at first hand.'

Sandy, perturbed, said nothing as Dunster continued.

'The American's name was Lee. He'd first seen the girl on the verandah. Having been passed ok by the old hag he became a frequent visitor and finally suggested that he take

Elmo with him on his business tour of the West Indian Islands. Well old de Lisle agreed, on payment of a lump sum down, which Lee said nearly broke him, but he was crazy about the girl! He even agreed to a weekly allowance in dollars to be paid to the alleged grandmother. One condition was that she be returned in good condition and not in the family way.'

'Good God!' muttered Sandy disgusted.

'Any way, my tale is not yet told. It gets meatier! When they got to Port of Spain the old hag wrote to Elmo to persuade her to improve their finances by lifting Lee's wallet while he slept and posting it back to her in Barbados. The girl succeeded in pulling the trick but Lee would never have suspected her except that old de Lisle found a Letter of Credit in the wallet good for any sum up to $1,000. She took it along to your Bank and the cashier promptly phoned the police!'

'Was she locked up?'

'Caused a bit of a palaver but Lee refused to prosecute. He sent Elmo back to her dear relative with a stiff letter telling Leila what he thought of her and that it was only his regard for Elmo, that they weren't both in the calaboose! Elmo returned to her verandah.'

While Sandy fulminated in silence, Dunster went on to regale him with various anecdotes of the girl and her quota of visitors, some accepted, some hurled forth with revilings by Grandma and not a few robbed while asleep while under the influence of her narcotic drinks. 'Which reminds me Jock, don't accept any drink unless the girl has one out of the same bottle!'

Sandy was beginning to think that Dunster's unrequited lust was making him exaggerate. He felt quite stunned by these frightful revelations and couldn't associate it at all with the exquisite and innocent-looking beauty he had danced with. It couldn't be true of this girl! He longed to see her to find out the truth for himself but afraid at the same time in case it was true.

But they were doomed to disappointment. The verandah was empty. The moonlight made it eerily forlorn; the gentle wind made the bead curtain over the doorway rustle musically. There were a couple of cane chairs and a small table on the verandah so they sat down undecided. At length Dunster said, 'I wonder if the old woman's around?'

They were both considerably startled when a deep contralto voice said, 'Yes, the old woman is around Mr Dunster.'

They turned in their seats and involuntarily got up to greet the very striking woman standing in the entranceway holding back the curtain with one hand with the other on her hip.

'Heavens!' muttered Dunster. Sandy, mouth suddenly dry, couldn't get a word out. If this was Grandma, she was certainly not a hag and not so old either.

'If you've come in the hope of seeing Elmo, she is not here and is receiving visitors no longer. She is out with her fiancé Señor Corazon.'

Dunster looked thunderstruck. 'Do you mean to tell me that Elmo Crofts is to marry the Venezuelan, Corazon?'

'I mean just that,' replied the woman. 'I think you two men had better come in and have a drink.' She turned and went into the bungalow.

'Come on Jock! This promises to be interesting!'

Nothing loth, Sandy followed him indoors. The room was comfortably, if bizarrely furnished, the style and colours somewhat startling, but they selected seats as the woman left them to presumably get drinks. Sandy had taken a seat near the outside wall and noticing a flap like that of a letter-box, he lifted it. It gave a good view of the verandah of course so was obviously where Leila viewed the clientele and bawled out the price list.

The woman returned with three glasses and a bottle of white rum on a tray, which she deposited on a small table and then seated herself opposite her two visitors.

'Help yourself and your friend and I'll have two fingers myself,' she said to Dunster who was gazing at the woman like a man in a trance. He jumped up, filled the glasses and handed the drinks round.

After a couple of sips, she again turned to him and began to rally him on his look of surprise on seeing her for the first time. 'What did you think I looked like you old scribbler? One of your Police Court cases I suppose?'

'Gran'ma…' he began apologetically.

'Don't 'Gran'ma' me. My name's Leila de Lisle, - Leila to you both if you are friendly.'

'But Mrs de Lisle,' he protested, 'you don't mean to tell me you are the same person we've all heard about as Elmo's Grandma, the one with the rasping voice that bawls through the partition?'

'The same,' answered the woman with a crooked smile. 'I can put on an act like the best of them. Haven't I been an actress for more years than I care to remember? Wasn't I on the boards in New Orleans, Para, Manàos, Rio and Buenos Aires?'

'So that accounts for it,' said Dunster. 'I must apologise for my evil thoughts. You certainly can put on an act Leila. But why take a part to your own detriment? Give me your life-story and I'll give you a build-up in the Bajan Gazette that'll put things right for you.'

'*Mille merciements, mon ami*, but I prefer to remain incognito. No publicity for me.'

Sandy had drunk the generous 4 fingers of rum Dunster had thought suitable for the occasion and was now feeling decidedly audacious. He was rudely studying Leila.

The light was poor, furnished by a solitary oil lamp but he divined her age to be about 60 though she held her years very well, he conceded. Perhaps it was the light or

65

Thunder's revelations but the handsome face did have a curious look of evil.

He thought perhaps she was Spanish or Portuguese by her high cheek bones and her thickly lashed black eyes. She was strongly built with olive skin and her oiled black hair was deeply waved but her nose was undeniably African. When she smiled, she showed perfect but quite large teeth, but the full lips held a sneer; sarcasm or cynicism, he couldn't decide which.

Watching her face, he realised that her dark eyes had strangely long lids. The narrowing of those eyes combined with the crooked smile were what made the face look evil, he decided. Still, she was good-looking and poised and very striking in a white satin frock with a quantity of gold jewellery. At least a dozen bracelets moved musically on her arms and her large earrings were set with green stones. They flashed in the lamplight, adding to her exotic looks.

Thunder and Lightning dished out some more rum and soon began edging nearer the woman and started stroking her bare arm, the satyr look pronounced on his pallid face.

'Leila,' he said in his rumbling voice, 'has anyone ever told you how beautiful you are?'

Leila giggled tipsily.

'Hey, cut out the smooging!' said Sandy revolted by the reprobate Thunder making love to this somewhat sinister female. Besides which she was old enough to be his grandmother.

'What about Elmo? Let's go along to the Beach Hotel and see if she's there.' He'd had enough and the woman rather put the wind up him.

He wanted to get a move on then and there but the large doses of rum had gone straight to his legs. He sat there as one paralysed and tried hard to focus on the discussion going on between the other two. His concentration kept slipping away from him in the most irritating way and just as he thought to try his legs again, he slipped into sleep.

He was wakened by Leila rubbing bay rum into his hair and temples and Dunster grinning and slapping at his face.

'Come on Jock, wake up! You've got to get home! It's well after midnight! I'm surprised a Scotchman like you can't take it.'

Sandy shook himself and after a glass of iced water obligingly pressed on him by Leila, he was sober enough to get on his bike. They wished Leila farewell and set off for Bridgetown. Wavering unsteadily at first Sandy had to take a good grip on his handlebars until the fresh air cleared his head.

Thunder and Lightning, being a more seasoned drinker seemed quite unaffected and sober, and whizzed along undeterred. Being so late they had no wish to collide with the night-soil women who were usually about their business at this time of night, swaying along with their huge trays of the stuff on their heads. They were in luck and saw not a soul. Thunder saw Sandy safely to the back gate at the Bank.

'While you were snoring your soused head off,' murmured Dunster, 'I gathered some interesting facts from Leila about a weird side to Elmo's personality which I'll tell you all about later chum. Nighty-night!' And with the parting grimace that passed for his smile, he pedalled off humming to himself, still full of energy. Sandy glowered after him.

He made his way into the silent building and headed for his room feeling somewhat nauseous. From the mutton and rum or Dunster's ghastly tales and advances on the de Lisle woman he wasn't too sure.

Thunder and his lousy stories, Sandy thought dismissively, entering his bleak quarters. For once, he was glad to get to his room and bed.

❧ Chapter 7 ❧

Leach announced one day that the three of them had been invited to become members of the Sabana Club.

'It's the one exclusive club in Barbados where you can meet respectable white people and enjoy a game of tennis in the afternoon. I strongly advise you to join MacNeil, it might keep you away from those niggers you're so fond of associating with.' Sandy ignored this remark, fairly inured by now to Leach's boorishness and low-brow mentality.

'Right-oh,' he agreed. 'I'll come up with you one afternoon. I'm always keen for something new.'

A few days later they went up to the Club. It was housed in an isolated building on the savannah that had formerly been the Guardhouse, long since abandoned by the army once garrisoned there. Many a soldier then had died from yellow fever as the graveyard testified, but that was far in the past. The stone army buildings which circled the grassy park had all long been converted into boarding houses and hotels like the Stafford.

Sandy's first impression was agreeable but unexciting. There were several quiet aloof Englishmen who made up the numbers at the Club but he did meet a few interesting characters both Bajan and English. A colour bar was in operation but many accepted white Bajans had coloured ancestry and, he discovered, they were at great pains to conceal it, often passing themselves off as of South American extraction. This rarely fooled anyone in an island as small as Barbados but was passed off anyway, with some secret scorn. Sandy privately thought the whole situation and attitudes both ludicrous and horrible in the circumstances, but it was very real.

But there was one member who was able to steer Sandy's energies into more reputable and indeed more elevating channels. He was one of the most agreeable members of the club, the Bishop, who simply loved rum swizzles and this put him and Sandy on a friendly footing straight away.

One day he found the Bish, a stout gentleman in his fifties, exclaiming over a copy of the Times. To Sandy's mild surprise he was looking at a familiar painting of a well-developed female in the buff with her rounded buttocks to the viewer, reclining gracefully and contemplating her face in a hand mirror; the Rokeby Venus.

'Velasquez masterpiece,' intoned the prelate with sonorous distress. 'It's outrageous! Attacked with a hatchet by some suffragette! Slashed several times no less! The National Gallery has only just acquired it too. Sacrilege, absolute sacrilege!' Sandy agreed and commiserated with him.

In the event, the voluptuous Venus, as women were invariably in the habit of doing, was in fact instrumental in giving Sandy's energies a fresh direction, for he and the Bish, who was sincerely fond of painting, now found a mutual interest in art.

This was something Sandy had always had a talent for so he was delighted when the kindly prelate introduced him to a couple of painters. One was more interested in mixing highballs and cocktails than in the pursuit of Art, Sandy discovered, when he was taken up one Sunday to the artist's studio in the north of the island. He had no quarrel with alcoholic refreshment; he felt he was already fully up in the arts of inebriation; but, he'd come to learn about paint. That whole encounter was a dead duck as far as Sandy was concerned.

Luckily the Bish also introduced him to a good painter in oils called Boon who had studied under an eminent teacher in Paris associated with the great John Singer Sargent. Sandy was highly delighted.

So, Sundays saw Sandy and Boon sallying forth very early with paints, brushes and sized paper to make oil sketches. For a young man constantly in the pursuit of diversion he knew it was good for him to find something that he could really put his mind to, and was in fact glad of it. They got on like a house on fire and notwithstanding the more elevated subjects of art and the modern artists, their trips were soon enlivened with tales of the bohemian life of Paris which was of course very much to Sandy's taste.

ও

As Aimée had predicted, he, Leach and Joyner had begun to receive a host of invitations from the 'best' people of the island. They duly attended dinners, bridge parties and tennis parties but these were soon a form of purgatory to Sandy.

The formality which so fulfilled the social expectations of the other two, Sandy found boring, not to say stultifying. Bajan society seemed immured in the past. Here they still stuck to Victorian prejudices despite the rather more liberated Edwardian mores emerging back in the London he'd lived in for a year before.

Bajan girls of marriageable age were strictly chaperoned; there was hardly opportunity even for the mildest flirtation. Conversation was stilted and mannered and mostly parochial in mixed company, which was not to Sandy's taste at all. The dinners were formal with the diners going in two by two, male and female. Like the animals in the Ark, he thought.

Even the tennis parties were restrained, the women by their long skirts and the men, thought Sandy, probably by their guilty consciences! He came to dislike their artificial posturing in front of the ladies. He was unsurprised that not

70

a few of them hit the high spots when their wives and sweethearts were in bed. As during Victoria's time there was a rigidly well-behaved side of life alongside a dissolute and immoral one. Although the dividing line was very thin, to the respectable, the profligate was rendered non-existent by the simple expedient of ignoring such behaviour, or even dismissing it from their minds.

But Barbados was such a small place that even the most innocent of young ladies got wind of any 'goings on.' News of course travelled almost with the speed of light thanks to the natural network provided by the coloured servants. Since everyone was on familiar terms with their servants and both dearly loved a gossip and a scandal it was extremely doubtful if the duplicity of the men folk was as consummate as they imagined it to be!

The result of all this social consciousness and prudent formality, made any socialising in mixed company seem very humdrum and since everyone was on their best behaviour, none of this suited Sandy, restless for distraction as he was. It struck him as being as artificial as a hothouse. These constant restraints of speech and behaviour irked him; his personal idea of *joie de vivre* seemed lacking in the various pursuits and past-times of Bajan Society.

To him these events were really a waste of valuable time, but not wanting to offend or make it obvious he soon made excuses at intervals to evade them before he got too heavily embroiled and his absence noticed too much.

He could only conclude that perhaps he wasn't a very respectable 'white'. He really was *not* cut out to follow their proscribed social round, he decided. He felt the pull of the other much more colourful side of Barbadian life. So far, he'd only touched the fringes of it and was therefore eager to make the most of what it offered. He admitted too that he didn't really want to keep away from it, in fact rather relished the disapproval he knew society would have if he was too obvious in his choice.

ℳ

Owing to his alleged knowledge of foreign languages, Sandy had been transferred to the Foreign Bills counter at the Bank. As a result of having no balance to strike, his working day was suitably shortened. With his natural bent for a good time this was hardly good for him. By four in the afternoon, he had one object in mind, to get his bike out and head for Aimée's house where he was sure to be made a fuss of.

He found them grand company and being beyond the pale in more senses than one, they had no restrictions of 'Society' behaviour to bother them. He was given a room where he could strip off and get into his swim-suit and then, arms linked, they would all stroll down to the waters' edge and plunge in with a lot of youthful shrieks and yells.

They taught him their sidestroke where not a limb is seen out of the water. It was very swift and elegant especially when used by the women, their sinuous bodies moving effortlessly through the water. When enjoying a lazy swim through the clear water they would face each other and talk comfortably of this and that, which he considered eminently pleasant and sensible too. He knew he was becoming thoroughly spoilt by these sybaritic interludes.

Sandy soon developed a becoming tan nicely cultivated under the gentler rays of the westering sun on his evening swims. But Aimée was not in favour at all; she wanted him to keep his skin white. Uninterested in what he deemed as just northern pallor, he thought a tan improved his looks no end; it suited his sun-lightened fair hair and hazel eyes, and moreover, set off his tropical wardrobe to perfection. Thus, despite her urging him to retain his whiteness, he made liberal use of tropical oils to that effect.

He was aware however that Aimée was very strict with herself to preserve her 'white' image. She exercised regularly too and watched her weight carefully, anxious to preserve her figure from the stoutness prevalent among middle aged ladies of colour like her maid Sadie, and so make her coloured blood obvious.

At Aimée's suggestion he kept a clean palm beach suit and all the necessary accessories in his room there so that he could bath and change after swimming and stay to dinner at any time. Afterwards he would relax in one of their comfortable chairs while Aimée sang humorous calypso songs or Lois played the piano and regaled them with 'Thora' or 'River of Years.'

Aimée was a witty and soignée hostess who looked very youthful despite being 40; Lois, sweet and unaffected and always as stylishly groomed as her aunt. They were both well-read and well-educated, thanks, Sandy learned to his delight, to the considerable money their father had made from his skills as a fisherman, especially from turtles, even supplying them to no less a person than the Lord Mayor of London, among others. Lois had enjoyed furthering her education and grooming in London for some years but loved and missed her Island home so returned to its sunny shores. In their interesting and charming feminine company, he was as relaxed and happy as a sand boy.

He'd been up to Hastings for a Saturday swim and gay dalliance with Aimée and Lois and was returning on his bike along the Bay road, when a buggy approached him from the opposite direction. As Sandy passed the vehicle, he felt the sharp flick of a whiplash in his face. He slewed sideways and braked hard to have it out with the occupant of the buggy. The driver had obligingly reined in the horse.

Sandy was taken aback to see the contrite face of a beautiful girl who was holding the reins and the offending whip.

'Dreadfully sorry!' she said in a soft voice, 'did I hurt you?'

'Not a bit!' I'm Sandy MacNeil, I'm from the Bank.'

'I'm Maureen Dare, How d' you do?' She proffered a slender hand. 'We've already heard about the new Bank men. News of people from England spreads quickly here.'

Surprised he hadn't run into her before, he shook the delightful hand with great pleasure and smiled engagingly at her, his hazel eyes taking in the creamy skin and large lustrous eyes with their dark lashes. Thick wavy hair cascaded from under a large shady straw hat tied under her chin with a broad lilac ribbon and she was sweetly dressed in a short-sleeved white muslin frock and was, he thought the very perfection of Barbadian beauty at its best and loveliest.

'Would you care to visit us?' she went on in her soft voice.

'With the greatest of pleasure.' answered Sandy trying hard not to reply too ardently and frighten her away. 'I'll come on a visit soon if I may?'

'Of course,' she said, a blush mantling her soft cheeks. She then went on to describe where her parents lived and how to get there.

They parted with firm promises of an early visit and Sandy watched her drive off feeling quite hot under the collar.

'*What* a piece of luck!' he thought, touching his cheek where the whip had caught him. Then he set off at speed to get bathed and changed for the evening as he was due to dine at some social luminary's house.

Now, he rejoiced, in meeting the lovely Maureen, there were more prospective delights ahead. And moreover, a further alternative to those formal social obligations he found so narrow and often oppressive. This proscribed colonial life seemed extraordinarily inappropriate he thought, in this island which was the very quintessence of passion and vitality with its sublime light, its blazing colours and hot sunshine. For himself he was both charmed and exhilarated by it all and meant to make the most of it.

❧ Chapter 8 ❧

One lunchtime, Sandy was checking to see if he had any post at the G.P.O. in Bridgetown, where letters could be collected from the glass-fronted post boxes there. As usual there was a crowd of people congregating in the courtyard in front. He was delighted to see the Golden Girl among them. She was looking so lovely he was quite unable to resist going over to speak to her even though he knew that both male and female Bajans would recognise and condemn the 'awful creature.' He was delighted to see she was on her own for once and very glad of the opportunity of drawing himself to her attention.

The female element of the Bajan better class habitually wore thick heavy veils with their hats to protect their skins from the sun. Sandy was getting used to it though one had to learn to recognise one's *vis à vis* by voice, figure or even the feet. Social contact in the town with these women was thus a tricky situation that Sandy considered somewhat farcical. But Elmo wore no veil.

She wore a Panama hat with ribbons and her hair hung in lustrous ringlets down her back. Her graceful neck was encircled by a necklace of carved pink coral roses, set off admirably by her glowing skin. Her organdic frock fell to the ankles, but the underslip beneath ended delightfully at her knees, so that her elegant legs were in full and seductive view. This alone was enough to condemn her in the eyes of all respectable women.

To Sandy the outfit was enchanting: he greeted her, smiling happily into the lovely face, his admiration clearly visible on his own. Looking at him with her tawny, slightly slanted eyes, and a smile on her lovely lips, she repeated the invitation to visit her and Ramon at the Beach Hotel one night. He assured her he would do so soon.

The following evening after dining with Aimée and Lois at their bungalow and relaxing with cocktails, Lois murmured.

'Sandy dear, it is not very wise to acknowledge Elmo Crofts in broad daylight in front of so many people. You will do your reputation no good by it.'

Sandy, frowning, turned his head to look at her, somewhat annoyed at the speed by which gossip had reached his friends. Neither was he enamoured of being lectured on his social behaviour either, however sweetly put.

'The bush telegraph has been busy,' he answered caustically.

'No kitchen gossip, dear. I saw you myself! You left her as if you were in a dream until a young man came up and spoke rather angrily to you!'

'Yes, the loathsome Leach. He asked me what the hell I was doing talking to that tart in public and everyone knows she's a bad 'un'.'

'He's not far wrong, Sandy dear,' said Lois seriously. I'm afraid Elmo is thoroughly bad. She was very troublesome at school. We were at the convent school together, she, Maureen Dare and I.'

'Oh! You know Maureen Dare!' he cried, momentarily diverted.

Of course I do,' she said. 'She's a friend of mine. But why the sudden interest?' she cooed, with a sly grin.

'I suppose you've heard that I've met her,' he replied, a trifle piqued, 'Bet that was on your tom-toms!'

'Don't be rude about the tom-toms dear. Maureen told me herself but I admit I felt very jealous when she said she had invited you to go to her place!'

'Don't be jealous, I wouldn't desert you two darlings. But you know me. Always keen for something new. I thought I'd go up there tomorrow night.'

'She'll enjoy that. Maur and I have been friends ever since we were at the convent school together, although I did return to England for a few years after that. But we've stayed friends as she has no side and doesn't mix with the 'best' people much even though she could. She lives quite quietly and is very sweet. She spends most of her pin-money on poor coloured folk, some of whom do impose on her goodness I'm afraid. I love Maur and it really wasn't the tom-toms, but dear innocent Maur herself who told us of the nice Bank boy she'd met, but we didn't reveal that we knew you.'

'When she visits us it's usually in the morning so don't be alarmed,' interjected Aimée, 'I don't suppose she leaves her daddy's bungalow after 7 o' clock in the evening unless chaperoned by Mama.'

Sandy got up and took Lois' hand in his and led her over to Aimée's chair, where he sat at her feet, drawing Lois down with him.

'Darlings, you won't lose me, I promise. You know I can't abide this colour bar. In fact, I loathe it. I am really happy knowing you. I love being with you and I hope we shall always be the best of friends! You are so sweet and loyal.' He held both their hands and looked at them fondly.

'Thank the Lord you are both so independent. It's rotten that you have to feel like this, and that white society looks down on you. It beats me why! You are intelligent and attractive women and damn it, a great deal more so than many whites! It really goes against the grain darlings that our association should be hidden away like this.'

'Sandy dear,' Aimée said, 'I don't want to appear cynical, but you haven't been here long enough to feel your feet yet. You'll soon be well-established with the élite, may even marry one of them. Then, I assure you, you will not give us a sidelong glance let alone wish to associate with us.'

Sandy protested vehemently. He was full of assurances that they meant more to him than that, aware that rejection by the whites really went deep with Aimée. How fortunate he thought that it was less so for Lois but her aunt plainly felt for the pair of them and their prospects.

He looked over at Lois who had got up and was now leaning on the piano with her arms folded. She looked so sweet in her white frock with some frangipanni flowers in her glossy black hair. With her little retrousée nose and large dark eyes, luscious lips and marvellous teeth she was a gorgeous picture. He caught a glimpse of her slim tanned ankles above her white satin shoes as she crossed her little feet and contemplated her toes.

'Anyway,' said Lois, sitting down at the piano and running her fingers lightly over the keys 'Maur is a much better person for you to be seeing than Elmo, Sandy.

'You know I have no colour bar, Lois.'

'It's not that dear. At school she seemed possessed of a devil. In fact, Mother Superior was convinced she was. It was through her that a young novice killed herself.'

'This is all very mediæval!' chuckled Sandy taking this with a good pinch of salt.

'No,' replied Lois. 'It's serious dear. The visiting priest said her real religion was Obeah.'

'Obeah? I've heard of that before,' remembering the ferocious Kate's mention of it. 'What on earth is it?'

'It's just an elemental jungle religious cult imported from Africa in the slave days,' replied Aimée in an indifferent voice. 'In Haiti it's called voodoo and is a real menace and used politically, but over here it is a very emasculate form of the original Ju-ju, just a lot of silly superstitions.'

Lois looked at her aunt in mock severity.

'Aimée. Don't pretend you don't know there is an Obeah House out at Black Rock!'

'Fiddlesticks,' said Aimée. 'You've been listening to Sadie. If you listen to servant's talk, you'll believe anything.'

'Hey, all this talk of jungle cults sounds very interesting!' cried Sandy, - 'and if there is an Obeah House, I'd like to see it!'

'Don't listen to that,' said Aimée quickly. 'It isn't very healthy. It's all about blood sacrifices, fetishes, duppies and zombies, and other things of which I only know the names.' She seemed disinclined to continue the conversation.

'*I* know all about Obeah,' declared Lois. 'I know all about Dumballa, Ogoun, Ezelee, the Papaloi and the Mamaloi…'

'Hold your tongue Lois,' cried Aimée sharply, distaste and annoyance in her usually tranquil voice. 'You'll give Sandy the impression we are straight out of darkest Africa! In any case I don't want to hear about these filthy superstitions. Where did you learn all this rubbish anyway?'

'Darling,' Lois giggled, 'I heard it at school from Elmo - she was an authority on Obeah! Didn't you know her mother was a Haitian woman and even her papa was keen on voodoo? She learnt it from them and frightened the nuns with it! They asked the visiting priest to exorcise her - I told you, they thought shc was possessed of the devil!' she said naughtily.

Sandy could see that Aimée was getting seriously put out, so decided to change the subject, promising himself he'd investigate this Obeah later.

Some time later as he was making ready to leave, they both made sweetly encouraging comments about his coming visit with Maur.

'But you *will* get seduced away from us Sandy dear,' they said, bombarding him with kisses as if they felt his defection was imminent. Lois' last kiss had a passionate intensity to it as if to hold him in the moment forever.

&

Full of anticipation on the following evening, Sandy made a perfunctory meal at the Stafford Hotel and cycled down the Bay Road and followed Maureen Dare's directions to her parents' house. It was easily found, and happily, lights glowed through the half open jalousies. It was a large white bungalow and was set agreeably in an extensive garden. He leaned his bike against a tree and went up the few steps to the verandah. He knocked gingerly on the door.

The coloured girl who answered the door gave him a gleaming look as if she knew who he was. The tom-toms undoubtedly at work, thought Sandy with an inward grimace as he followed her in to be announced.

He entered a large well-furnished room and was greeted by a tall thin woman whose evening frock did nothing to enhance her lean body. She introduced herself as Mrs Dare, Maureen's mother.

'Is Miss Dare in?' he asked diffidently, rather disconcerted by the woman appearance.

'She'll be along in a moment. She's just changing her frock, - probably in your honour,' she replied with a thin-lipped smile. She moved over to the gramophone in the corner and selected a record. 'Shall we dance while we wait for her?' Without waiting for a reply, she put her selection on and started it playing. It was a paseo.

Sandy instinctively did not care for Mrs Dare nor wished to dance with her, but it was impossible to refuse. Still, dancing was preferable to the kind of stilted conversation that he felt would ensue, going by this dry woman's uncompromising mouth and odd manner.

They started the one-step and she moved easily but she seemed far removed from what they were doing, so her timing was faulty. As they moved with the rhythm, Sandy found the thin body under his hands very unappealing, so hoped Maur would make her appearance very soon. One dance was all he felt he could tolerate.

When the record finished, to his intense relief, Mrs Dare moved away.

'I feel tired tonight somehow,' she said languidly. 'Let's sit down.' She indicated a chair for him and sat down herself on a long settee and leaned tiredly back into the corner.

Sandy looked at the woman's pinched face and the thin hard line of her lips. They were compressed as if in pain. Her half-closed eyes were heavy-lidded and deep in bruised-looking sockets. The make-up she wore gave her face adequate colour but her exposed neck looked sallow and unhealthy. She bore no resemblance to Maureen that he could see.

As if divining his thoughts, she roused from her lethargy and looked at him rather fixedly.

'I'm not Maur's mother you know. I am her step-mother. Maur's mother died at her birth.' She said no more but continued to regard him.

Hoping his relief was not too plain and therefore the cause of her studied silence, Sandy was nevertheless caught by the fixity of her regard. He noticed now that her pupils were widely dilated. He remembered that amongst his warnings of divers tropical hazards, his doctor father had spoken to him about such things. Mrs Dare was undoubtedly under the influence of some narcotic. Morphia? What had got her into that, he thought curiously.

To his profound relief, Maureen suddenly entered the room.

'I'm sorry to keep you waiting, Mr MacNeil,' she said with a lovely smile.

The sight of her sweet femininity was in such striking contrast to the other woman that he felt an overwhelming need to cast his arms about her to imbibe some of her warmth.

'Your mother and I had a dance to pass the time. Shall we dance too?' he asked, hopeful of this excuse to hold her in his arms.

She was dressed in powder blue the colour of her large and starry eyes. A tiny wreath of real flowers was entwined in her dusky hair and the generous smiling mouth showed her impeccable pearly teeth. She was enchanting, he thought as she assented demurely.

'Allow me,' he said and put on a waltz.

As they danced, his hand lightly clasping her slim waist and with her cool hand in his, he could not but contrast his feelings with those when he danced with the exotic Elmo. With her his senses reeled and his pulse beat faster with sensuous excitement. Here was purity and tranquillity, the very fragrance of Maur's body was chaste, her creamy skin exhaled a faint and delicate perfume. As her soft hair lightly brushed his cheek, he wanted to hold her closer from sheer delight, but dared not breach the code of etiquette especially under her silent mother's cynical gaze.

They danced a little and talked for a while but Sandy made his excuses fairly early, as he felt ill-at-ease in the presence of the smouldering-eyed Mrs Dare, who naturally stayed as chaperone throughout and evidently didn't trust him.

As he was taking his leave, a rather grim-visaged man with a dark lined face came in. He ignored Mrs Dare completely but greeted Maureen and introduced himself to Sandy as Mr Dare, her father. He then stumped off into the house with a muttered excuse. Sandy left.

Kindling his oil lamp and wheeling his bike into the road, Sandy paused irresolutely. Queer couple to be associated with that angel, he thought, looking back at the silent house. No wonder she spent her time helping out coloured folk.

Yet despite the strange home set-up, Maur's gentle and uncomplicated company offered a sweet aside from the temptations of the heady tropical delights he so enjoyed and the stuffy protocol that made up most of his social life. Seeing more of her would be an undoubted pleasure, he decided, as long as he didn't become completely unnerved by that frightful woman and her somewhat grim chaperonage.

The heavy scent of some tropical flower near the gate assailed him as he set off, bringing Elmo sharply to mind and his promise to get out to the Beach Hotel. Mm, he mused, it's time I made the push to shoot out there and see what's what. With that resolve in mind and pleasant thoughts of the lovely Maur jostling with thoughts of seeing the delectable Golden Girl again he headed back through the warm night to his spartan quarters at the Bank in a speculative and agreeable haze.

❧ Chapter 9 ❧

A few evenings later, true to his resolve, Sandy cycled out to the Beach Hotel. He'd been told it was out past Hastings on the road to Worthing but lay off the main road and faced the Caribbean Sea.

Soon he came upon its bright lights seen plainly through some trees and heard the faint sounds of a dance band. With some excitement, he pedalled down the narrow road in the direction of a staccato rendering of the rumba, the pebble-filled maracas tapping out the rhythm. Although the hotel was a blaze of light, the crowd and South American Band were all on the dance floor set outside as usual, under the stars. It was surrounded by little tables, all fully occupied and busily attended by perspiring waiters.

He shoved his bike in the shed provided, which was already close to bursting point and sauntered over to join the throng. Knowing it was one of Dunster's haunts, he found a waiter and asked if he was around. He indicated the newspaperman sitting alone under a tree. This had a ladder set against its trunk that led far up into a roofed-in platform high among the branches. Dunster was in the dinner suit that badly needed renovating and his tie hung down un-tied over his shirtfront. He looked three-parts sozzled.

Sandy took the seat opposite him and proceeded to fix his tie for him.

'What's with the Swiss Family Robinson out-fit above you in the branches?' he asked.

'That my dear Mac, is for the convenience of customers who wish to make love in seclusion and I have booked it in the hope of using it this evening. What's your poison?' He signalled a waiter.

'Whisky.'

'And a gin frappé for me,' he said to the waiter.

'My dear chap' said Sandy. 'You look depressed enough already. Gin is a wholly depressing drink. Try some scotch.'

'It's not the gin that depresses me,' said Thunder and Lightning, 'it's that!' and he waved his empty glass in the direction of a table some little distance away.

Sandy jumped. There was the Golden Girl with Ramon Corazon and they were making love to each other with their eyes.

'I fail to see why that should depress you. It's a lovely sight.'

Through the strains of the rumba, Dunster's deep bass tones boomed out,

Like Elihu, the son of Barashel the Boosite, of the kindred of Ram, my wrath is kindled and I am constrained to speak.'

'Nice quotation Thunder, but why select Job at a moment like this?'

Dunster vouchsafed no answer but leaned heavily on the table and gazed with glassy eyes in the direction of Elmo.

'And dost thou open thine eyes upon such an one, and bringest me into judgement with thee. Who shall bring a clean thing out of an unclean? Not one!'

The rumba had stopped in the middle of this quotation with the result that Dunster's booming voice declaimed like a Victorian preacher's, to the considerable astonishment of the surrounding drinkers.

'That's great, Thunder, let's have some more! I like the contrast. Rumba, booze, Boosite and Job!'

'Listen Bonehead, that night you passed out at Elmo's I had from the de Lisle a few recorded events from the life of Elmo Manchineel Crofts, that'll make your hair stand on end. I know she is a naughty girl, but I find she has some hereditary evil in her make up that makes her a jinx, - a *very* un-lucky person to have dealings with!'

'That shouldn't worry you old bean, you haven't a nickel's chance for any dealings with her.'

'No but you might, after Corazon,' he said sarcastically, 'but I shouldn't like any dear friend of mine to come to a sticky end.'

'You are talking rot!' Sandy laughed.

'Well let me tell you what I had from Leila. Did you know Elmo was at the convent school here?' He laughed harshly. 'That's where the fun started. When she was about fourteen.'

The drinks arrived at that moment. After taking a quick refreshing gulp he leaned his bony elbows on the table, eyes gleaming from the combination of gin and what he was about to relate. Sandy prepared to enjoy his whisky and Dunst getting into his stride.

'Our lovely Elmo began to take what appeared to be epileptic fits, but after each fit, she would divest herself of her clothing in full view of the shocked, but delighted girls, talking rapidly in an unnatural voice - sometimes a piping falsetto and then in a voice as deep as a man's baritone.'

Thunder's voice rose and fell in a parody as he got into full flow. 'Some of her ravings were gibberish but every now and then she spoke clearly in English making the most atrocious allegations about the nun's conduct with the visiting priest, a handsome young Irishman called Father Timothy. As you can imagine this brightened up convent life no end! At first the girls sent for one of the sisters but in time they found Elmo's displays so interesting and amusing and finding she was none the worse after them, they attended her séances in force and finally did their utmost to keep the staff out of it.'

'Dunst you old idiot! This is tripe!' interjected Sandy.

'No, no, my innocent babe. Listen and learn! The girls knew when to expect these exhibitions, as they appeared regularly once a month, but in between, Elmo had other highly amusing things to show the girls. How to dry frogs and toads and even small snakes and send them to people they didn't like with suitable descriptions of the mode of death the receiver was likely to suffer. In addition, she had several prescriptions for love potions. Very diverting to the adolescents in love with Father Timothy! Anyway, some informant apprised the holy father of Elmo's behaviour and that intelligent and resolute priest, who had already on more than one occasion, surprised the girl 'tout nue' giving one of her exhibitions, was determined to get to the bottom of her distressing complaint. The celibate priest was in a worse predicament than St Anthony! The sight of the precociously developed body of this golden girl racked his very soul, so with bell, book and candle he attempted a spot of exorcising, but the devil would not be cast out. In fact, a little devil got into poor Father Timothy for he found himself looking forward to the monthly manifestations and kept surprising Elmo more and more!'

'How on earth do you know all this Dunst! Don't tell me you are a confidante of the reverend father!' Sandy exclaimed. 'Or is this just your overactive imagination you old toss-pot?'

'Kindly don't keep interrupting!' rejoined Dunster and gulped enthusiastically at his drink, 'I'm just getting to the climax! The priest had recourse to the medical profession,' he continued, his pale face gleaming dewily with gin and the warmth of the night. 'and with the Reverend Mother's approbation, called in his friend Dr Kilcoyne. The physician diagnosed the girl as an hysteric and prescribed bromide three times a day and a firm hand. Neither alas had the least effect on Elmo's exhibitionism. Little wonder. An observant pupil found a collection of strange looking nuts in Elmo's locker, which proved on examination to be none other than Kola nut, a fruit which contains a powerfully stimulating drug. On questioning, she failed to reveal the source of her supply.' His eyes gleamed wickedly in his dewy face.

'Hang on Dunst old chap. I need another drink to cope with all this!' Sandy interjected, scowling and looking sceptical, and waving to a passing waiter.

'Well pin back those lugs! We now get to an interesting turn of events old man! This troublesome girl then formed an attachment to a young novice called Faith, under whose influence, Elmo modified her behaviour to a certain extent although she still had her monthly attacks of hysteria. Elmo's affection for the novice increased in intensity however, so much so that the pupils reported having seen them kissing like lovers. Mother Superior rose in her wrath and said Elmo Crofts must go, and immediately! This precipitated a scene in which the two girls protested that they could not endure parting, howling and weeping copiously. In the midst of all this emotional mayhem, Elmo's father died - but in fact, this advanced matters, because Leila de Lisle turned up as guardian and came to arrange for the removal of her charge, - to the great relief of the religious community anyway. And then,' said Thunder in a sepulchral voice full of emotion and alcohol, 'came tragedy! The night before Elmo was due to depart, there was a stormy scene between her and the novice Faith in the novice's dormitory where Elmo had really no right to be. Elmo returned to the girls' dormitory pale and shaken and shortly afterwards a despairing shriek was heard and the heavy fall of a body in the courtyard forty feet below. Faith had jumped from her window, but she was already dead when they picked up the broken body.'

'What a horrible story, Thunder! Are you sure you aren't drawing on the viler aspects of your imagination?' asked Sandy, revolted by the tale. 'Where do you get all this ghastly stuff?'

'It's my job saphead, I have a nose for a good story! You'd be surprised what people can't wait to tell me!' he grimaced. 'Leila included!'

Sandy looked across the dance floor at Elmo, strikingly beautiful, and lovely face attentive to something Corazon was saying. She looked up and caught Sandy's eye and flashed him a dazzling smile of recognition that gave him a strange pang in his breast. He grieved that one who was the embodiment of luminous physical beauty should have anything to do with such dark and more than unsavoury deeds.

He watched her as she danced and less and less was he inclined to take Dunster seriously.

'I think I'll go and ask Elmo for a dance,' said Sandy.

'Wait, 'said Dunster, 'I haven't finished yet and I must get it off my chest, or bust!' He took a gulp of gin, draining the glass.

'What? Is there *more* of it?'

'Yes, and worse to come' he said morosely, 'and this is where Goops comes into the picture.'

'Old *Goops*?'

Dunster nodded. 'Goops has a lousy habit of listening at his wife's door when she is enjoying a visit from her father confessor, Father Timothy, and he overheard the reverend father relating his difficulty to dear old Mrs Goops and entreating her motherly advice about the sinner Elmo, whom neither priest nor doctor seemed able to rescue from eternal damnation! A few nights later, Leila de Lisle was flattered to receive a visit from the distinguished anthropologist, - not that Grandma was keen on anthropology, but he looked rich. He wooed Elmo with a wad of notes and a quart of champagne and signified to her great relief, that it wasn't bed he was after but as a student of the races, he was interested in her Haitian ancestry and the things her ancestors were perhaps accomplished in, namely fetishes and Obeah. The girl stalled at this, a bit frightened that the old vulture meant to make trouble for her.'

'Now,' continued Dunster gesturing wildly to a waiter, his empty glass clasped in a bony hand, 'to continue. Father Tim is a friend of mine so I had a word with him. He tells me that Elmo was no dud pupil at the school. She was in fact a most intelligent student and would have gone far if unhampered by her evil side. She used to borrow books on religious subjects from the Reverend Mother but alas, far from influencing her beliefs to the good as the kind lady believed, she never lost an opportunity to pick holes in Catholicism and argued with Father Timothy about such things as The Immaculate Conception and the Virgin Birth until he was distracted trying to find convincing answers. Leila also tells me that along with the deceased Mr Crofts belongings, was a whole library of books, mainly dealing with strange cults like Voodoo, Obeah and necromancy. In her spare time, of which she now has plenty, Elmo pores over these books and makes copious notes.' Thunder grinned. 'The evil trend of the Professor's mind appealed to Elmo, - you know how he can talk, - and after he'd plied her with champagne, she started to show off and really staggered the old bird with her knowledge of Obeah and other cults.'

'What good is all this dabbling in demonology going to do to that girl. Somebody ought to get her out of it!' said Sandy in a rage.

'Yes, but who?' said Dunster refreshing himself from the new supply of gin appearing at his elbow. 'But worse is to come. Leila says that when Elmo has one of her manifestations, erroneously called 'fits' she disappears to Black Rock!'

'Wait. I've heard that there's an Obeah house out at Black Rock. Where is it anyway?'

'Black Rock is a place, my dear Mac, that I do not advise you with your faculty for nosing, to visit! If you don't get your throat slit, at least your pocket will be! There is a rumour that Elmo has been taken up by the votaries of

Obeah and installed as High priestess or Mamaloi of their temple, some wooden joss house out at Black Rock. Some grisly 'doings' go on when she's there on her monthly visits.'

'Well, what are we waiting for? Why don't we get a shilling ticket and go look see what's going on at this joss house?' said Sandy facetiously, fast taking all this with a pinch of salt.

'Fathead! The Obeah house, being a strictly illegal establishment, is more difficult to enter than a Masonic Lodge. Also, very few people know its exact location anyway.'

'Thunder, I find you enthralling and I want to hear more sometime, but if you'll excuse me, I'll ask this High Priestess for a dance.'

'I'll come with you. I need a closer look at the divine girl even if she is up to her neck in voodoo.'

'That neck is only made for the tenderer arts, it's far too beautiful for anything else. Leila must have enjoyed having such a worthy audience you chump. It just suits that lascivious mind of yours.'

They got up and went over to Corazon's table and after excusing themselves to the Venzuelan, Elmo and Sandy took the floor with a tango and Dunster occupied her vacated seat.

Having got a safe distance away, Sandy murmured in her ear that he wanted to see her some night soon, he couldn't wait any longer.

'Sandy dear,' she said 'I'm dying to have a long talk with you, and you can make love to me afterwards if you like, but I want a chance to convince you that half the things you are probably hearing about me aren't true!'

'You witch!' he replied, 'How do you know what I'm hearing about you?'

'I was watching you. Dunster's vehement expressions and goggling eyes, and your look of misery and glances in my direction conveyed a lot. Pure deduction dear. No witchcraft in it!'

'Oh Elmo! If only I could get you to give up all this irrational rot. Damn it all, if you really have some debbil in you, I'll exorcise it myself!'

She leaned back from him as they danced and surveyed him mockingly.

'Darling, I believe you could exorcise me if you tried really hard! But seriously, Ramon is off on some mission to Trinidad next week, so call in one night at the bungalow after dinner and we can discuss my trouble then.'

'What about Leila? If she splits to Ramon, he'll probably shoot me!'

'Don't worry about her. She knows I'll put a fetish on her if she starts anything. In any case if you want to make love, we'll go up to Pine Hill in a buggy. There's a lovely view from up there and I don't care for making love indoors anyway.'

Considerably delighted and excited by this invitation Sandy put his all into the dance. As the tango came to an end and they made their way back to the table, Elmo whispered, 'Now, I'll expect you without fail!'

Chapter 10

To Sandy, his work at the Bank was fast becoming an irksome interval between his quests for pleasure and excitement. Luckily, he was able to work quickly and accurately without much effort. The Chief Cashier expressed his approval, which mitigated it somewhat, but he always felt impatient for the end of the working day.

One morning on an errand for the Bank, he saw by a sailing list, that Corazon had departed for Port of Spain. In some excitement he returned to the Bank. There he found a note on his desk. It turned out to be an invitation to a supper and dance at the house of a well-to-do planter.

Blast, he thought. How can I get out of it? At lunch-time, he found that Leach and Joyner had also had their invitations. They were looking forward to it.

'Where the devil do you get to these nights?' asked Joyner

'Studying ethnology,' replied Sandy.

'Good Lord! Collecting moths?'

'That's entomology, you chump. Ethnology is the study of races.'

'I see, 'said Leach with heavy sarcasm, 'black races. But let me warn you old man to pay more attention to the white race or you'll find yourself transferred to Antigua, St Kitts or some other branch of the Bank.'

'Okay, I'll come to your dull dance,' Sandy said.

'Not so dull' said Joyner, 'a friend of yours will be there, Maureen Dare.'

'Oh! So, you know her, do you?'

'Yes, we know Maureen alright,' said Leach. 'We've met her at several houses recently. Always discretely chaperoned by her Ma or her cousin Atholine of course. See what you're missing with your ethnology?'

'You're right. I can't let a couple of mugs like you get away with Maureen. How did you know she was a friend of mine?'

'Well, I hate to tell you,' said Joyner, 'but she keeps asking where you are.'

'Thanks for the tip, Joyner. I've been rather busy of late. I'm glad she hasn't forgotten me.'

Here was a cleft stick and a half, thought Sandy. Not a comfortable spot. One half of him longed to see Maureen, the other called to Elmo. Perhaps I can manage both, he thought.

The supper dance was held in an old house, one of the showpieces of the island. A house so strong, that neither age nor hurricanes could destroy it. The original owner, a 17th Century pirate and notorious wrecker was an Englishman. He had made his home as English as possible, even to fireplaces and immense wall mirrors. The idea of a homesick pirate seemed rather novel to Sandy as he wandered through the rooms.

He had dressed himself with especial care that evening in his best evening clothes with a white jacket instead of a tuxedo. He viewed himself with some conceit as he passed the huge mirrors even though they had darkened with age. Looking around at the throng and recognising some of the Bank officials and their wives, he made himself properly evident, with Leach's warning in mind.

Several presentable girls were in attendance and it wasn't long before he espied Maureen and her chaperone. He made a bee-line for them and Maureen introduced her cousin, Atholine Anstey, a tall good-looking woman some years older than Maureen with an air of frustration as if the chaperonage irked her. Sandy wasn't surprised. But she looked resolute all the same. He speedily took Maureen off to the dance floor.

They'd enjoyed a few dances and were in the middle of a paso doble when Sandy asked Maur if they could meet other than at her home.

'Is there a chance for a little privacy Maur? Otherwise what I have to say will remain forever unsaid.'

She blushed adorably and smiled. 'Alright then.' She looked up shyly. 'I visit my Granny every day. I'll write you and we can meet at her house one afternoon. How will that do?'

Sandy agreed, mentally hoping that Granny was senile and stone deaf if she was to be present all the time. His few visits to Maur so far had been closely chaperoned, so all conversations and dancing had been overseen by Mrs Dare, which had cramped Sandy's style considerably. It had also kept his visits frustratingly short as Ma Dare's brooding presence was highly disconcerting and somehow inhibited him further.

While he was dancing with Maur, some of the other fellows kept cutting in, in the American fashion, which annoyed him no end. He soon tired anyway of the formal behaviour, the protected females, the propriety and the conventional dancing so he was getting restive. He stole glances at his watch since time was wearing on, and he didn't want Elmo to get tired of waiting and go out to one of her low haunts.

He asked Atholine if he could have five minutes on the verandah with Maur. She agreed to ten, so out they slipped. A glorious sight met their eyes. The landscape and sea were bathed in a lunar light that seemed so much brighter in this part of the world. Far out in the bay, they could see the waves pounding on the coral reef and could hear the wind susurrating enticingly through the leaves of the tall cabbage palms.

'The old wrecker who built this place used to tie lights to those palms on dark nights to lure passing ships.' said Maur conversationally, leaning on the balcony. 'They thought they were riding lights on ships in harbour and ran onto the reef poor things. He had his crew of ruffians rush out and attack the defenceless ships, murdering everyone on board and stealing the cargo and everything else they could find. Such a wicked way to make money!' she said in her soft voice.

'Charming fellow! But dear Maur, in such a lovely spot as this, it's only you I'm interested in. I'd rather talk about you.' He reached for her hand. 'I really came out here to tell you that I'm very much in love with you.'

'Silly! You've only just met me! And what is more to the point,' she said with gentle reproach, but not withdrawing her hand, 'I have been wondering where you spend your evenings that I don't see you at the houses I meet Leach and Joyner.'

'I plead guilty dear sweet Maur. I've just been looking round for excitement. No wickedness in it though, word of honour, but if you'll see more of me, I'll devote all my time to you. That'll be excitement enough.'

'Alright then, we'll meet at my Granny's soon, I promise,' she said giving his hand a little squeeze.

'Time's up.' said Atholine appearing on the verandah. 'Sorry to intrude, but you know what it is, reputations and all that.'

'A lot of rot, I call it!' said Sandy crossly. 'I couldn't even have kissed her in the time!' Both girls laughed and turned in the direction of the ballroom.

'I'm staying out here for a while,' he said rapidly deciding to pretend to be annoyed and so not accompany them back to the ballroom. He'd made up his mind that as soon as he had a clear field he'd slip away.

In no time, he was speeding away on his bicycle like the wind, making for Elmo's white bungalow, his heart pounding with anticipation. He could hardly believe he was going to get her all to himself and actually have the chance to make love to her.

He arrived at Elmo's in a state of high nervous tension. In this heightened state it was a considerable shock to see no sign of her. The verandah was deserted. His heart sank.

Somewhat at a loss he propped his bike against a post. Then, he saw a faint light coming from inside the house. Heart racing, he went on to the verandah and stepped gingerly through the door into the gaudily furnished room. A single oil lamp revealed a large bowl of the dreaded manchineel flowers conspicuous on a table.

'Hst,' he whispered, hoarse with apprehension. 'Anybody home?'

'Come inside here,' called Elmo's voice 'and what's all the whispering about?'

Hastily he entered the next room, which proved to be a bedroom, dimly lit by another oil lamp. His heart seemed to leap in his chest as he beheld the Golden Girl lying on her face on an elegant divan, a Brazilian cigarette between her fingers. Her thick chestnut hair fell about her shoulders and lay along her back. Through the thin fabric of her ninon frock, the curves of her young body gleamed tantalisingly in the light by which she was reading a book.

'Hello Elmo. I've left the élite purposely to see you.'

'I know,' said the witch, not looking up, 'you got tired of the conventionality and thought you'd like to give free rein to your natural instincts, isn't that it?'

'What are you reading?' he asked lamely, disconcerted by this forthright aspersion on his motives. And somewhat piqued by the rather discouraging welcome.

'Black Magic if you want to know,' she replied 'and please don't look so scared. I won't eat you because you are an hour or two late. I know you have your social obligations. Sit down,' she added, patting the bed invitingly.

He sat beside her and at once became acutely conscious of her nearness by the exotic perfume from her body.

'Where's Leila?'

'I've sent her down to Maxie's for a bottle of scotch and if I know her, she won't leave till she's thrown out. Let's hope she meets Dunster and then they'll take hours tearing my character to pieces.'

'Have you got a drink darling? I've been drinking iced watery claret till my insides are frozen.'

She bent down to a cabinet by the bed and with a conspiratorial smile, drew out a bottle of Black and White and two glasses. She poured out two good drams and got up and returned with two knobs of ice, which she plopped into the drinks.

'*Salut amigo,* 'she smiled and clinked glasses, '*con choce.*'

'Cut out the Español' he said sulkily, 'I'm not Ramon.'

Elmo helped Sandy off with his white jacket and threw it on a chair. Putting her arms around him she snuggled against his chest.

'No, you're not Ramon. You're not a bit alike darling. He's rounder and softer. You're hard, like steel, I like that,' she sighed dreamily. 'Even your hair is quite the opposite, smooth and the colour of gold, Australian gold!' She giggled naughtily. 'Like some sovereigns an Aussie once gave me. I still have some left and when I first saw your hair darling, I thought of that gold.' She reached up and smoothed his fair head. 'Quite unlike Ramon's curly black locks. And,' she added chidingly, 'while Ramon's voice is soft and caressing and full of passion, yours dear Sandy, is so stern and aloof! Just as if you've made up your mind that you won't let yourself go!' She gave him a tantalizing smile.

'Thanks for the odious comparison.' he said, throwing her back on the divan and covering her parted lips with his mouth and kissing her passionately. She responded with equal passion and expert use of her tongue and arching of that slim soft body against him. Sandy felt himself drowning in the sensations that her kissing and her warm flesh moving against him through the thin material, were rousing in his own. Aroused already, his body responded with a great rush of pleasure and he covered her face and neck with kisses, his senses swimming with the fragrance of her skin and the silky texture under his lips.

But even as he was carried along by the joy and delight of his hands on her rounded flesh and felt her body respond to his touch, he was nevertheless aware of a troubled sense of the decadence, the sin and darkness of the black arts that shadowed her beauty. While his body ached with desire, a little nagging voice in his head urged him not to get carried away, not to give in.

Elmo, sensing his slight restraint, employed her considerable arts with hands and mouth to break down the barriers she felt in him. Trembling with arousal, he yet managed to break from her passionate embrace. He lay back on the divan, his mind seething with a troubling mixture of visions of the body that moved so passionately against his, naked with Ramon, or jerking with religious frenzy in some ghastly orgiastic black magic ritual.

Elmo sat up agitatedly. 'Sandy! Sandy. what is it? What have I done?' she asked beseechingly. 'Do I repel you? - Don't you care for me after all?'

'Elmo!' he said earnestly. 'I'm mad about you and I want you, dear God I want you! But I can't get this black arts stuff out of my head! I can't make love to you properly with all this going round in my mind. I don't think I *can*, until you give up this obsession for Black Magic you seem to have. It's ugly and evil! I can't help it, it's just here between us! We need to talk about it! I need to think!'

'Oh! Any excuse is a good excuse,' she said bitterly. 'You are a bit unfair when I'm prepared to take *you* at your face value! You have no other value you know!'

'Thanks! You mean I have no money to burn like Corazon!'

'If you like,' she replied tartly. 'I need money and I need love, lots of it. Perhaps you prefer the charms of Lois Dance or Maureen Dare. Maur, nice girl that she is, looks to me as if she's straight out of the ice box!'

'I mean nothing to you anyway Elmo,' he said, piqued, and annoyed by these peevish remarks. 'You just want to add me to your list of lovers. Why can't you be content with one man? You're an intelligent human being yet you behave like a strumpet.'

'Isn't that what brought you here – certain expectations? My wild reputation?' she asked dryly.

'I came because I couldn't resist seeing you. You are so damned fascinating Elmo. The thought of making love to you was irresistible. That's all I could think of. But all that ju-ju stuff and Ramon and your other lovers got into my head and spoilt it all. It's all so damned immoral.'

'I refuse to be annoyed. I do behave in an unorthodox way, but that's because I have worked out my own philosophy, so I must put up with being insulted by you and the others who criticise me.'

'I'm sorry Elmo. I shouldn't be so critical,' he replied, 'after all it is your own life. But all that rot Dunster fed me, revolts me. I don't think I really believed it. But then, there you were, reading a book on the stuff and I - well - I just couldn't bear the idea - and all that rubbish about Ramon and his curly hair for God's sake! - It puts a chap off, - and anyway, I'm jealous and want you all to myself.'

The girl turned on her face again and began turning over the leaves of the book on Black Magic.

'Perhaps if I told you my version of Elmo Crofts, or Mancinella as my father called me, and about Ramon, you would understand a little for me,' she said. She left the book and sat up on the edge of the divan.

Love-making now seemed out of the question, so Sandy sat up beside her and touched her hand.

'Yes, please tell me Elmo. I really do want to know darling. It's driving me crazy.'

'I've only had a very few lovers, Sandy.' She pushed back her tumbled hair. 'It's been my way of seeking for the man I feel I can live my life with. So far Ramon is the nearest to my ideal and in addition, he has made me a very attractive proposal.'

'Yes, he's asked you to marry him, hasn't he?'

'Yes. Men don't offer me marriage darling; - Ramon is exceptional. But it's still only in the event of a certain mission being a success.'

'That's a bit tough. I remember. He talked of some mission when we first met. We all toasted it in champagne.'

'It's very dear to his heart Sandy. But it's very dangerous and *I* think, foolhardy. In his own country, Ramon is a lawyer and belongs to the intelligentsia. They've all been hounded out of the country by Gomez, the present Dictator, who is a full-blooded Indian with a whole harem of wives and employs an army of thugs to do his dirty work. But he hates Ramon's class and resents their influence. One of the exiled intellectuals, a man called De Castro, lives in Paris and has appointed Ramon to contact all the other exiles who are living in various Capital cities all over Europe and elsewhere. He's supposed to collect funds to buy arms and stage a counter-revolution back in Venezuela. That's what he's working for right now. In fact, he has thousands of rifles and machine guns bought in Germany and lying here in the Customs at Bridgetown. But, for shall we say, diplomatic reasons, the Governor here has put a prohibitive tax on each gun. So, Ramon is hanging around here, trying to get a reduced levy on them. But he's also making plans for the coup with his agents in Trinidad and on the mainland. Now you know what took him to Port of Spain.'

'Great Scot, Elmo!' he cried, instantly diverted. 'And this is really about to happen? It's extraordinary!'

Privately, Sandy thought all this sounded thrilling and it made his blood tingle, but Elmo was plainly worried by it all.

'The worst and maddest part is that when the revolution is ripe, he plans to enter the palace and assassinate Gomez himself! I fear for him and I've tried to concentrate and prophesy for him, but I have somehow failed to get through to the Loi, to the Mystere.'

'The Loi? The Mystere? Then it *is* true, you do go to the Obeah house at Black Rock?'

'Yes,' she said simply, 'it's true.'

A chill passed over him and as the bead curtain rustled in a sudden little wind, he immediately felt afraid in the semi-darkness of the exotic room. Elmo must have seen the sudden fear in his eyes and felt the tension in his body for she laid her hand on his chest as if to soothe him.

'*Soyez tranquille*,' she murmured, 'don't be afraid darling Sandy. The powers of evil cannot harm you while I am here.'

'Don't talk like that Elmo! Evil has nothing to do with someone young and beautiful - it's impossible. I won't have it!'

'You know nothing about me Sandy.' She moved away from him.

'I know all about the powers of evil. I've been trained in evil! I'm steeped in evil!' she whispered fiercely. 'The powers of darkness are all around me for *I* am Evil! Evil itself!'

'What are you saying Elmo! This is appalling,' cried Sandy, horrified.

Suddenly she sprang up from the divan and stood with her back to the wall, half lit by the lamplight. Thoroughly alarmed, Sandy recoiled and stared at her as she faced him, her eyes dilated and fierce.

'Look Sandy! Look at me! Don't you *see* how evil I look? Evil! Evil!' She threw back her head, her hands tangled in her tawny hair, her voice rising in a throaty cry. The edgy flickering of the yellow lamplight made dancing shadows over her body in its almost transparent dress, alternately revealing and concealing the lovely body beneath. Sandy caught his breath in both excitement and rising alarm.

'No Elmo! No! Not that ugly word! You could never be evil!'

This was horrible. This must stop. He forced himself to speak calmly.

Darling, you're just a beautiful girl! The Golden Girl, - like, - like your manchineel flower!'

'Aah! The poison flower!' Her voice dropped. 'Yes Sandy. Just like me. Touch it and you burn! '*Arbol de la muerte*', the tree of death.' Suddenly all the fierceness left Elmo's face. Now her golden eyes held Sandy's gaze in a look of such sadness that he involuntarily reached out to take her in his arms.

'No, no. Wait,' she pushed his hands away, 'I *must* tell you who I am!' she said pleadingly. You must hear me. You must believe me. I know that in your church you speak of the Élite of Heaven, well Sandy, I am the Élite of Hell! - let me finish! - I carry the hereditary evil of my mother! She was a fetish woman from Haiti. She inherited her voodooism from *many* generations of it in our African blood. There is *no* hope for me, Sandy. Every cell in my body is permeated with it!'

Her voice held a sob and she shook her head. 'I don't know how far back it goes. My father was white, yes, but his whole life and mind were taken over by her and the cult of Obeah. All my childhood, I ate, drank, slept, dreamed, absorbed Obeah from him. I have been very skilfully trained in all the dark arts and practices I assure you! I have a whole collection of books and ancient writings that he left me, to prepare me for my role of hereditary Mamaloi, a high priestess of Obeah, a Snake woman!'

'Look,' she cried and with a sudden gesture tore down the strap of her frock baring her left breast.

With a sharp intake of breath, Sandy started up.

'Good God! Who drew that horrible thing? Who did that to you?'

There, perfectly tattooed, gleaming vividly green in the lamplight, was a snake entwined round the delicate pear-shaped breast with its sleek head pointing to the rosy nipple.

Elmo didn't answer. She covered her breast again, her eyes downcast. 'Every month a Loi enters and takes possession of my body and I must go to the Obeah House to make my manifestations and prophesy! Sandy,' she cried, her voice plaintive, her eyes filling with tears, 'there is no escape for me! I am possessed of a devil and no-one can exorcise me!'

She sank onto the floor, her hands covering her face where she broke into a flood of passionate weeping. Sandy went down on the floor to her and cradled the distracted girl in his arms, kissing her hair and soothing her until the stormy tears lessened.

Summoning up all the cold Scots reason he had, he appealed to her intelligence, pointing out the fallacy and foolhardiness of it all and urging her to simply reject this superstitious stuff with contempt and loathing. She had only to be willing and determined to renounce it, he urged, since the hold it seemed to have on her distressed her so deeply. He couldn't tell if any of it meant anything to her or the words were just merely comforting, but at least she became calm and quiescent in his arms.

They then sat together on the divan, but she still clung to him.

'You know, darling. I don't really love Ramon, but I do like him very much and he is very kind and generous. He doesn't know I'm a snake woman and when he said that after the revolution, he would take me to Venezuela and marry me, I was very grateful to him. Perhaps the attacks will leave me and I won't need the Obeah House any more. Ramon said he'd be made Minister of War and that I shall be someone of importance. He says that I am educated and intelligent enough to carry off the position. Wouldn't that be lovely Sandy? I'll ask him to get you a Bank if you like!'

'No fear. I hate Banks! He can make me Minister without Portfolio if he likes with a large salary and a bevy of beautiful girls. That'll do me!'

They both laughed and her mood lifted. Seeing that now she was getting the better of her distress, he felt it was also time to leave; both were still really occupied with their own confused thoughts. Kissing her goodnight, he promised to see her again soon and left her, a dark solitary figure on the verandah.

With the dawn of another day, he experienced a strong revulsion of feeling and tried to concentrate on his work. He found it difficult. Despite strenuous efforts his mind kept returning to the previous night's fiasco and the unhappy and sinister revelations about the Golden Girl. What should have been thrilling had left him repelled instead. Normally applying himself to his work single-mindedly and proud of doing it at speed, he was annoyed to find his equilibrium was right up the creek.

That day it was his turn to accompany a shipment of gold to the docks for return to London. The Negro porter came in and said the buggy was waiting and with a big grin, indicated a box on Sandy's desk. It was of unstained pinewood and about nine inches long and eight inches high. It looked innocuous enough, so he went to lift it. To his intense surprise and chagrin, it didn't budge an inch. The porter grinned even more. The cashier came over and told the porter to buck his ideas up and get the box out to the waiting buggy.

'That box,' said the cashier, contains exactly 5,000 English sovereigns and I don't advise you to attempt to lift it MacNeil, it takes the porter all his time to do it.'

'Is that so!' said Sandy, thoroughly incensed. He raised the box sufficiently to get his fingers under it and slid it across to take the considerable weight on his stomach muscles. Followed by the jeers and encouragement of the staff, he just about managed to stagger out to the waiting buggy and was very relieved to get the thing onto the floor of the vehicle without actual injury. Never again, he thought sardonically, knowing that it was his black mood as much as pride that had pushed him into being such a blithering idiot!

Getting up into the buggy, he was then handed an antiquated pistol and with the porter as bodyguard, he departed on his errand. Since the porter was full of cheap rum and the gun looked useless, he sincerely hoped they wouldn't be attacked on the way. From the many facetious remarks called out to the porter about the contents of the box along the way, it seemed that most of the population of Bridgetown were fully aware of his errand. The sublime idiocy of the whole situation then struck Sandy as decidedly humorous, and his spirits lifted involuntarily. This was a British Colony and thankfully gangsters as such didn't exist here. All the same he was glad to deposit his shipment at the Shipping Company offices without incident.

Being out of the Bank and with the colourful bustle and noise of the town around him always raised his spirits. He realised ruefully that he enjoyed being out of the Bank more than in it.

He cast about in his mind for a vocation that would give him more freedom and began to wish he could seriously pursue a career as an artist. He couldn't think of anything else that would answer the purpose, so in the meantime he decided to call in at The Ice House for a John Collins to cheer himself up and make the most of his temporary freedom before going back to his bills and books.

✑ Chapter 11 ✑

The revulsion of feeling against his lower instincts remained to unsettle him, so he decided to spend his days in more respectable company. He attended dinners and bridge parties, and dullish dances which at least were enlivened by Maureen's presence, although with cousin Atholine diligently in attendance. Moments alone with Maur were irritatingly confined to the briefest of brief intervals. Sandy felt sure Atholine counted the minutes personally. Not from malice, but nervous of the conventions, she was punctilious to a fault.

Thankfully, it wasn't long before he got a letter from Maur to tell him he could see her at her Granny's. Alas for Sandy's hopes, she was neither senile nor stone deaf. She was a dear old lady in full possession of her faculties and never left Sandy and Maur alone for one instant. She made it plain she was quite in favour of them being friends, but soon let Sandy know that she had heard from various sources that he had a taste for low company. That she thought to wean him from it seemed evident in her encouragement for Sandy to come to her delightful place over-looking the sea at Worthing. And being a good soul, and of a religious turn of mind, kept handing Sandy strident tracts of a condemnatory nature depicting the fate of the evil-doer. The wages of sin in these tracts were indeed writ large - and in detail!

However, Sandy's new intentions to lead a more exemplary life were helped along this narrow path of good behaviour much more by his own somewhat ingrained sense of Calvinist guilt and sin. It was this that made it possible for him to cope of late with the bridle so firmly held in the hands of white society. It was certainly sweetened by Maur's lovely albeit chaste company.

Meanwhile, Joyner had become engaged to some Bajan sugar merchant's daughter so wasn't so much in evidence. Leach hadn't been so fortunate in that direction. Probably, thought Sandy unkindly, his *acne rosacea*, now nicely inflamed by the climate, had something to do with it. Leach had been glad to see, as he sarcastically put it, that Sandy had given up his study of ethnology.

One night after an evening at the Dares, he was just turning in to the side gate that led to his rooms above the Bank, when he was accosted by a skinny red-leg of about seventeen, in a ragged frock and bare feet.

'Gamin rouge, one shillin' mistah?' she wheedled.

Just then, around the corner came One-Eyed Dan, an immense policeman on a huge chestnut horse. One glance at Dan and the girl flew. With his great bulk straining at his blue uniform and topped by his huge white helmet, he struck terror into all frails, petty criminals and evil-doers alike.

'Dem red-legs too much trouble Mr Mac.' Dey always 'roun' here lookin' fo' trade off de schooners an' drunks. Doan you touch 'em. All got woo-man sickness!'

'Don't worry Dan. My father's a doctor and he warned me all about it. Goodnight.'

'Good night sah,' and Dan wheeled his great horse round and made off in the direction of the red-leg. Sandy grinned. Dan was a great character and Sandy, instinctively drawn to larger-than-life characters and eccentrics of all kinds was naturally drawn to Dan. He had spent some of his spare time listening with great enjoyment, to Dan tell his tales of his young days at the harbour and the fights he'd had with sailors and smugglers. It was in one of these fights that he'd lost his eye and, he said, made him fit only for chasing wharf-rats as the red-legs and coloured girls were called who infested the wharves to ply their trade in the oldest profession.

Dan had however made himself famous, though to some, infamous would have been a more appropriate epithet, by his self-devised method of announcing the death of Queen Victoria. With a large brass handbell and mounted on his huge chestnut, he had thundered through the night, clanging his bell and bawling out the dismal news and rousing the bewildered citizens from their slumbers with his stentorian voice. The Colony had certainly logged it as unforgettable.

Chuckling to himself, Sandy went up to the top floor and, as was often his custom before going to bed, went to look out at the peaceful night scene in the Careenage and the schooners swaying gently at their moorings.

Suddenly he heard a low whistle. There below on the wide verandah was Leach in his pyjamas, signalling to the ragged red-leg who had skirted round the block and returned to the wharf. Leach then disappeared and in a very short while she was inside the gate and Leach was leading her into the bath house.

Well, well! mused Sandy. Who's the student of ethnology now Leach? He already knew Leach for a confounded hypocrite, as he took a good drink on the sly, so now it was coloured girls too. Not the best mode of research though old chap, he thought.

He made no mention of it, but a week or so later he found Leach quietly blubbing over his morning figures.

'What's up,' Sandy asked. 'Got the guts-ache?'

'Can't concentrate.' he snivelled.

'Here, give me your figures.' and Sandy totted them up for him.

'There's something on my mind Mac,' he said. 'If I tell you about it, you won't blow the gaff on me, will you?'

'Well, out with it. Been committing the unpardonable sin have you?' remembering the adventure in the bath house.

He looked mournfully at Sandy, his eyes red-rimmed and desperate. 'I've got the clap!' he whispered.

'Hell!' Sandy said horrified. 'That's bad! You'd better see Dr Johns the Bank doctor, chum!'

Sandy filled him in on the salient facts of the disease if he was stupid enough not to get treatment, though he knew from his father just how vile these methods were. He kept those intimate details to himself however, not wanting to set Leach off snivelling again or stop him seeing the doc.

'Oh hell and damnation!' he whispered, 'I'll get the sack!'

'No you won't, you're not the first, old man, believe me! With the Bank's ruling that junior employees are not allowed to marry, it happens. Obviously, we are supposed to be content with masturbation, or sublimate our libido with Sunday school or the Band of Hope! Anyway, one of the older clerks has had it twice and the doc 'fixed him up proper' according to him.'

This cheered Leach up enough for him to go to the doc for treatment. Alas the treatment put the poor patient through agonies of pain and distress with the primitive medical answer to venereal disease, with syringing with caustics and the ingestion of loathsome medicines. Complications were the rule rather than the exception and a condition known as chordee, where the poor afflicted member remained as hard as a rock until it could be persuaded to lie down again, was one of them. Poor Leach paid for his illegal passions in blood, sweat and tears.

One night he wakened Sandy, imploring him for advice on how to deal with his chordee. He wanted to treat it with iced water, but Sandy told him that hell no, old chap, the only thing was warmth! Leach needed a lot of convincing that this really was absolutely essential. To cheer him up while he dealt with his distressed organ, Sandy told him about a lad well-known to the girls of the Flag Hotel, who rejoiced in the name of Right-Angle Jack.

'One of the girls,' Sandy said in a cheery voice, 'told me that the lad once had an attack of chordee which he failed to reduce and got into such a rage from the pain that he struck it with a poker, fracturing the muscles of the organ! Ever after that when he had an erection, it was at right angles; hence Right Angle Jack! Very popular I believe.'

Leach dismally failed to see the humour of this little anecdote. For many days he spoke of broken bottles and fish-hooks and a desire to bite on a tree when he went to pass water. He didn't get the sack as anticipated, but was transferred to San Fernando, Trinidad.

With his departure and Joyner, the personification of respectability in attendance on his affianced love, now moving out of Sandy's orbit, he had the feeling he was no longer under observation. This was not good for him especially as he was chafing badly at the circumscribed life he had been leading. The other freer, colourful life of infinite variety on the waterfront was drawing him like a magnet.

Thanks to his assiduously good behaviour, dear Granny had relented enough to allow him and Maur to sit out on the verandah while she remained indoors. This gave him the chance to steal furtive kisses and brief embraces. But this merely increased Sandy's frustration. He needed to find an outlet for his energies. He needed to feel free.

He tried everything he could in the way of respectable diversion. The best sellers of the day, 'Three Weeks' or 'The Woman Thou Gavest Me', kept him occupied but briefly and his rooms at the Bank drew him not at all.

He visited the cinema-cum-theatre and there he found the antics and excited chatter of the natives in the audience as amusing as Ben Turpin. During the showing of dramatic films an American was hired as interpreter of the unfolding scenes. Rising to the occasion he enlivened the proceedings with such descriptions as 'De guy holdin' the bunch of plants, approaches the dame with the idea of a little neckin' but she deals him the dead pan when the flat-foot shoves his head in at the windah'. But nobody seemed in the least enlightened by these somewhat obscure interpretations but clapped him with thunderous enthusiasm at the end of every picturesque discourse.

Sometimes they had real live plays and players. Bridgetown did have a real treat when Frank Cellier brought a barnstorming company out from England and regaled the audiences nightly with Shakespearean offerings from Macbeth to Richard Three Eyes, as it was fondly called and Sandy was happy to be part of the enthusiastic audiences. Their visit was quite an event and the company were even entertained at Government House.

But nonetheless, he kept making forays into 'enemy territory' on the waterfront. Escaping to some of the lower haunts, Sandy encountered some of the entourage of another distinguished visitor; Theodore Roosevelt was on his way to do some exploring in Brazil. Heaven knows where these chaps were recruited from, Sandy thought. They were hefty lads, and hard drinkers, mad on girls and dancing. One he saw out at the Beach Hotel was still in his black jacket, striped trousers and knobbly-toed boots and danced and drank for hours in this rigout sweating like a bull, much to the amusement and amazement of the more lightly and comfortably-clad revellers.

Sandy was momentarily diverted when a dispatch appeared in the press later from Theodore, announcing that he'd discovered an unknown river in South America, which prompted the English explorer, Savage Landor to write a sarcastic letter saying that it had been discovered years ago. Sandy thoroughly enjoyed the ensuing mud-slinging in the papers between the two, each calling the other, some kind of a liar.

But none of this really took his mind off his frustration at those sweet brief embraces with the lovely Maur, or worse still, his infatuation for Elmo.

Partly through a spirit of rebellion, and partly through wanting to catch any sight of her, he threw himself into a round of nightly revels in the grog shops, bar rooms and dance halls from Bridgetown to Black Rock. Full of abounding energy, he was easily caught up in the frenetic life of the Waterfront.

He knew he was being escapist, but the alternative, that of the rounds of careful respectability, held little real appeal. To Sandy in his restlessness, it was too irksome. The formal constraints seemed incongruous to Sandy in this lush vibrant paradise of relaxed manners. Even the fact that he had to keep his charming visits to Lois and Aimée sub rosa galled him. At least he could relax there. He found far more enjoyment and outlet for his zestful energy and untrammelled taste in the warm, colourful, lively company he found outside Bajan society. Naturally, it called to him.

He looked for Elmo everywhere.

Ramon, on his return from Trinidad, had hired a decent buggy for Elmo, over the back of which was draped a large expensive-looking fur rug he'd brought back from his travels.

Sandy grew to identify her cab by this rug that hung a foot or two down the back of the vehicle. He grew to dread it too. He often met them driving along the roads at night. They would always wave and call out friendly greetings but his heart was heavy, his body too with longing; he desired her intensely. The memory of her yielding body haunted him and frustrated him. So did his oppressive distaste for that other, darker side of her. This further prohibition in fact, intensified his physical yearnings.

Sometimes he would meet them out at the Beach Hotel and dance with her and talk to Ramon. He told Sandy of his intention to make Elmo his wife and establish her in a position befitting her beauty and intelligence. The irony was, that Sandy liked and grew to admire Ramon, almost to the point of hero worship as they discussed the problems in his beloved country and the solutions that were so dear to the hearts of her scattered exiles.

One mad night, Sandy begged him to take him with him.

'I'm strong,' he said eagerly. 'I can shoot. I'm used to fire-arms. I've stalked deer in the Highlands of Scotland, I can stalk men!'

'I admire your courage mi amigo, but our quarrel is not yours Mac and think of the repercussions it might entail if you were killed and I had encouraged a British Citizen to take arms in a revolution!'

'I hate the restricted life here. Have you any idea what it's like? And back home in Scotland, come to that. You should try a Scots Presbyterian Sunday! I'm fed up with it Ramon, I need action and adventure!'

Ramon smiled and sympathised, then added.

'Besides, my dear boy, don't you read the papers? I am amazed at the complacency of you English! Germany is ripe for an excuse to destroy your Empire. Don't you think that rattling their sabres at the French by sending in that gunboat to Agadir is a pointer?'

'Oh yes, the Agadir Incident, all that nonsense over Morrocco with the Germans and keeping them out of the Mediterranean and breathing all over Gibraltar. That's settled surely - but like most of my countrymen,' Sandy confessed, stoutly Scots but momentarily acceding to being British for the sake of argument, 'I'm afraid I don't trouble my head about international affairs, but I do admit that some articles warning against Germany's intentions by Robert Blatchford and Lord Roberts have given me some qualms.'

'Both are soldiers,' said Ramon, 'and know the trend of events. You'll be in a war of your own before you know where you are.'

He was to remember this conversation later, when many weeks before any certainty of war, German nationals began to move homeward from South America.

He met many passing through Barbados *en-route* for the Fatherland. He met them where the fun was fast and furious, in the Flag Hotel, dance halls and bar-rooms.

There were all types, a chemist, a professional wrestler, a teacher, a mining engineer and many like them: from all walks of life and with some frenetic fun in view before travelling on home to Germany. But then diplomats didn't frequent the waterfront. They were all too la-di-da to mix where they might get real information, he thought later. Too busy getting ulcers from insipid food at official banquets and sipping tea in drawing rooms, far removed from real life and real information. Their stupidity was our tragedy. But these bitter thoughts were later, when he was up to his eyes in mud in Flanders and so many of his overburdened men fell and drowned, held inexorably down in the quagmire by the weight of their full packs with too few of them having the strength to haul the fallen out of the deep treacherous mud. And the world went mad in 'a war to end all wars.'

❧ Chapter 12 ❧

One night out at Bob Teach's Select Bar and Dance Hall, Sandy was in close conference with an American Skipper from the Amazon who was relating to Sandy, ever a ready and sympathetic listener, that he was the means of his wife drowning.

He was being beguiled by Jansen's sad tale when Leo blew up to their table, resplendent in a Panama hat with his college ribbons, a vivid bow tie of many colours, a silk shirt under a blue suit with a broad white stripe and a splendid pair of black and white American shoes.

'A very good evenin' sah!' he greeted Sandy with an expansive smile. 'Forgive intrudin', but I wan' to see you fo' long time bout de party comin' up, but I be busy man now. I got taxi business!'

'Beat it nigger!' growled Jansen, 'beat it while the goin's good!'

'Hold on Skipper!' remonstrated Sandy. 'This chap is a college-bred Barbadian. I know him. He's a good fellow. Let him join us for a bit!'

Jansen scowled and said he only knew niggers as good for booting on the deck; he said he didn't know niggers were college-bred anywhere.

After some argument where Leo held his own, Sandy was at last able to engage him in conversation.

It seemed that Leo only wanted to tell him that he had been booked to provide two cars for a swell party that was coming off soon and he would reserve another for Sandy and his party if he'd like to go. It was to be at the opening of Bob Teach's new Hotel out at Speightstown; selected guests would have free house, liquor and food. Teach was tired of the waterfront and wanted to strike out as a first-class hotelier at Speightstown as well.

'Da home of his ancestor!' added Leo.

'Don't say he's a descendant of *the* Teach, scourge of the Spanish Main Leo? Sandy grinned 'The one with his whiskers tied behind his ears with a ribbon before going in to action, who smoked sulphur and ate broken glass for breakfast?'

Leo's gleaming teeth flashed in a wide grin. 'Well Bob is his descendan', only he doan tie his whiskers and only smokes cigars!'

'Promises to be a good night, book me in! Thanks Leo!' exclaimed Sandy, delighted at the prospect.

Leo pushed off with a cheery adios and Sandy was left with the Captain and his remorse.

'Well, looking at old Bob behind the bar I've often thought he was the perfect prototype for a pirate,' said Sandy, looking over at Bob's swarthy face with its black beard and the gold ear rings which he said he wore for his eye-sight.

He got on famously with Bob. He'd told Sandy how he'd been many years at sea, but after an unfortunate incident with the U.S. Customs he'd retired and bought the Select Bar. If anyone started developing a desire for any rough stuff with Sandy in the bar, he would leave everything and showing his white teeth in a diabolical smile at the offender, he would indicate that Sandy was a friend of his, so what? This often saved Sandy a lot of argument and left him free to enjoy his drinks or company, male or female.

Jansen had by now consumed a lot of gin and now, his anguish was so great he said, he just had to tell Sandy the facts. He was a stubborn man, an obstinate man, he said, probably inherited from his Swedish ancestors. He used to live in Seattle and sailed a small yacht as a past-time. He sailed in fair weather or foul with his wife who came from sea-faring stock. One day he told his wife to get ready, they were going out sailing. She reckoned a bad squall was blowing up so she didn't want to go sailing. That rattled him. She must, simply must go sailing with him!

Jansen ran his hands agitatedly through his thick blond hair, and continued. Afraid of his temper, she had agreed. The squall broke when some distance out to sea, the yacht heeled over and capsized, entangling his wife in the rigging. He tried desperately to free her, and failed. She went down with the little craft. He swam ashore alone. The anguished sailor then sold up everything he owned and worked his way by stages to the Amazon, where he was working off his salvation on a dirty old tramp steamer. He had tasted of the dregs of Manàos, that once wonderful city with its operas house, its boulevards reminiscent of Paris, 1,000 miles up the Amazon where evil was at a premium and virtue at a discount. He drank heavily, consorted with all sorts of women, but he could not efface his wife's memory.

He stopped to rummage in his wallet as drinkers do at a certain stage to show photos of wife and home. Sandy looked at him candidly. He was, he reckoned, about 40 and apart from some signs of over-indulgence and some grey in his thick curly fair hair, Karl Jansen was still a handsome fellow. After some effort, Sandy coaxed him out of his abject gloom and suggested he accompany him to somewhere more home-like than Teach's Bar. Jansen agreed, so Sandy called a cab and being in the mood, directed the coachman to take them to Aimée Dance's bungalow on the Hastings Road.

They found Aimée reading and Lois as usual at the piano.

'Don't you two girls ever go out?' he asked as he introduced Karl to them.

'Very seldom darling, unless to a few friends of our colour,' replied Aimée. 'But needless to say, we are delighted to see you Sandy, and your friend,' she added, smiling graciously at them both. She excused herself and went out of the room to return with a tray of drinks.

Karl couldn't keep his eyes off her and having already relieved the considerable burden on his soul and consequently cheered up, smiled brightly at her as she offered drinks. Aimée in her turn seemed attracted to the American, so Sandy left them talking and joined Lois at the piano.

'Who's your new friend?' she whispered.

'A good-humoured American drunk with a murky past I picked up in Bob Teach's,' he whispered back.

'Good Lord, you do pick some choice company dear!'

'Don't worry, he's alright, I'll give you the details later. He and Aimée seem to be getting on like a house on fire. Let's you and me go for a midnight bathe and leave them to it?'

Nothing averse, Lois intimated their intention to her aunt. They prudently withdrew to go and change into their swimsuits, Sandy surprised and delighted that she had so readily taken him up on his suggestion. They met on the beach.

It was a lovely tropical night and the beach was quite deserted. They wandered hand in hand down to the edge of the sea hissing softly as it met the sand. It was dark and moonless but lit by a myriad of stars.

'Have you ever swum naked?' asked Lois suddenly.

Yes, often. In Scotland on a deserted beach.'

'Well, this is a deserted beach, isn't it?' giggled Lois softly. 'Let's really enjoy ourselves!'

'Suits me,' said Sandy entranced.

'No looking then!'

They separated in the darkness and Sandy threw off his costume and made for the water. Lois showed up in the starlight as a pale glimmering figure. She looked utterly desirable. He was quite deeply tanned by this time but not so his mid-section and was momentarily unaware of how this showed up as he took a few steps towards her. She fled towards the water and plunged in, splashing playfully then swimming off strongly. After a mighty exertion to catch up, he swam alongside her, the phosphorescent bubbles surrounding and following them both.

They swam in silence for a while, their eyes now fully accustomed to the dark. He reached out to take her hand and then breast-to-breast they swam lazily on their sides, the twinkling phosphorescence all about them. Sandy found it extraordinarily erotic and was almost beside himself with both arousal and joy. With a sudden swift movement and his superior strength, he turned Lois and made for the shore. Her thick raven hair floated around her, framing her pale oval face and as they got to the shallow water, Sandy reached for her and kissed her salty lips. Lois made an effort to wriggle out of his clasp, reproach in her large dark eyes.

'Mac, Mac! Stop! We've got to think!'

She stepped aside on the sand and bent over to wring out her long hair with her hands. The sight of that lovely young body gleaming in the starlight, her breasts thrust forward as she bent to her task, was too much for any Calvinistic resolutions Sandy had left.

'Darling Lois, you are adorable! Come here!' he murmured reaching out for her. He pulled her into his arms and they sank to the soft sand, still warm from the heat of the day. They lay locked together in mutual ecstasy at the contact of their bodies moulding against each other and still damp from the sea. They kissed passionately and then tentatively caressed each other as the tide ebbed and the stars lit their faces as they looked at each other intrigued and eager.

Suddenly, Lois gasped and struggled to sit up.

'We must go Sandy! Aimée will be getting suspicious!' She leaped up and grabbing her costume made all speed for the house.

Reaction set in for Sandy and he shivered. He found his swimsuit and pulled it awkwardly over his damp body, gritty with the sand clinging to it. He made his way slowly up the beach to the back steps. He then had to wait shivering in the cool of the alleyway till Lois came out of the bath house. She emerged still naked but with her sable hair now fluffed dry and almost concealing her. Sandy made an attempt to put his arms around her, but with a provocative slap, she eluded him and dashed for her room.

Bathed and freshly dressed in a white flannel suit, he returned to the verandah and was soon joined by Lois. She nestled up to him in her soft white frock and as he held her to him, he soon realised she was wearing precious little else.

You little vixen! he thought getting all aroused again.

'Strange silence from the lounge,' remarked Lois in a whisper. 'Let's have a look!' They went over to a point in the jalousies where they could peep in. Aimée and the captain were on the settee; she was ruffling his blond curls while he lay back with a look of ineffable bliss on his usually gloomy countenance.

'Lois, we have no right to eavesdrop,' Sandy whispered, turning her away. 'Let's go somewhere where I can tell you how much I love you,' he said softly against her ear. He kissed her, his body urgent against her yielding one. With a little breathy giggle, Lois took his hand and led him quietly to her bedroom.

They lay down on the bed in the darkness. With Lois' pliable young body cuddled against him Sandy could feel the wild beating of her heart under his hand as he cupped a firm full breast.

His own was beating a wild tattoo by this time at the exquisite pleasure of it all. He could feel her little nipple harden under his fingers and excited them both further as he nuzzled it with his lips through the thin material. Passionately kissing her eager mouth, he soon realised she was as aroused and ardent as he was. For Sandy the floodgates were open and with Lois' sweet fervour in response to his passionate kissing and stroking, all restraint went between them and they with-held nothing in their youthful disregard for the consequences.

In the aftermath of passion, and the sweet young body of the girl lying naked in his arms, Sandy suddenly felt scared and ashamed.

'Lois, it's getting late,' he whispered. 'If Jansen isn't coming, I must go now.'

They dressed quickly and returned to the verandah. Peeping once more through the jalousies, they were astonished to see Aimée and the Captain exploring uncharted seas in the amative line.

'Goodness!' cried Lois in a startled whisper. 'What on earth is Auntie doing in all the world? She ought to be ashamed!'

'They are older than we are darling and probably not so easily satisfied,' Sandy said softly, taking her hand and moving to the door.

With a final embrace he left her there, and like a criminal fleeing from the scene of the crime, bent to his wheel and tore along the road homeward, a prey to conflicting emotions but all the same aware of a tremendous release from the restraints he'd been under from his physical cravings for Maureen and failed unconsummated passion for Elmo.

It was with his brain still whirling and his emotions considerably disturbed that he saw Elmo's distinctive buggy drawn up at her white bungalow. Both she and Corazon were alighting from it. He was hailed and drew up himself. Accepting an invitation to join them for a drink on the verandah, he sat down with them at the little table.

Leila was in bed so Elmo did the offices. Ramon lifted his glass in salute.

'Amigo mio, it will not be long now. My appointment with Señor Gomez is about due.' His eyes glowed as he leaned back and his smile gleamed in the lamplight. 'Everything is ready; my preparations to free my country are complete. I leave for a secret point off the Venezuelan coast in about a week!'

Elmo put her hand over Ramon's.

'I wish I were as confident as you are Ramon.' Ramon took her hand to his lips.

'I can only wish you the best of luck, Ramon, and I still wish I was going with you,' said Sandy. 'We must have a farewell party before you go.'

'A party is already being planned,' said Elmo with a more cheerful air. 'We spoke to Leo at the Flag tonight. We are going to the opening of Teach's new hotel on Saturday night and Leo is going to provide a car for us and drive us himself. All we need is to get a few friends together, so dear Mac, we'd love you to come with us!'

'Splendid, I'd love to! Leo told me all about it. Naturally I agreed to come. It sounds as if it's going to be a good night. Just name the time and rendezvous!' Sandy grinned happily.

Settling the place and time to meet, Sandy finished his drink and bade them adios. Once again, he mounted his bike and set off. The interlude with his friends had broken the tension within him. His churning thoughts were now replaced by Ramon's forthcoming venture. That, with the vision of its dangers and the fun to be had at the forthcoming party out at Speightstown were a perfect distraction. He slept the sleep of the just after all that night.

❧ Chapter 13 ❧

Over the next few days, Sandy followed his usual routine at the Bank, his mind full of the fun that promised to ensue on the coming Saturday. Teach was ever a good host so the party was bound to be something special.

That evening, taking even more than usual care with his appearance, he set off for the Select Bar and the rendezvous with Elmo and Ramon, hoping that Elmo would be dazzled by his sartorial elegance and careful grooming.

Much to their delight, Leo arrived with a car that looked like a racing automobile. The car looked to be all engine. Jennie and Sadie were with him and with three more people to fit into it, the car's small body was going to be tightly packed. Sandy couldn't help but notice that the brown paint barely concealed the original gloss of the fawn beneath. Hot off the streets of Brooklyn, no doubt, thought Sandy. So, this was Leo's new occupation - dealing in stolen cars!

Sandy found himself wedged in between Elmo and Jennie and having already had a few rum swizzles at the Select, he felt he didn't care who he sat next to, whores or otherwise. Elmo contrived to insinuate her hand into his trouser pocket and the warmth and activity of her fingers soon awakened a very lively desire for her. Ramon was deep-sunk in thought, probably of his uncertain future and Jennie and Sadie sang 'Alexander's Rag-time Band' into the night air.

The coast road to Speightstown, some twelve miles away, was packed already with a stream of guests of both sexes, black and white. Mostly of the underworld but also any Bajans willing to risk their reputation, or what was left of it. Cycles, buggies, and dogcarts careered along to the opening of Teach's Hotel for free drinks and food. They had all taken to the road in one continuous stream, even crowds of people traipsing along on foot, all on the look-out for something for nothing and all the fun to be had on that promising night.

With the car's superior turn of speed, Leo soon passed everything on the road. He reckoned that judging by the crowd on the way, if they didn't get there soon, they would never get a room, far less a drink. Leo put his foot on the juice and his hand on the horn.

At last, they drove through the gates at the back of the yard, not surprised, after their speedy drive, to find that they were practically the first there. Leo took the precaution of parking nearest to the exit, with necessary foresight, he said; they never knew, they might need a quick getaway.

They found Bob in his new bar, which he had lit up with festoons of gaily-coloured electric lights. He was surrounded by hundreds of bottles of every conceivable kind of liquor as well as hogsheads of rum and beer and about a dozen husky Negro assistants and strong-arm men, in case of a rough house. His eyes gleamed happily above his black beard and his gold ear-rings flashed in the coloured lights as he greeted them.

Arming them with a number of bottles of scotch, rum and gin and platefuls of sandwiches he gave them a key to one of the rooms on the first floor. He warned them to lock the door if they wanted any privacy at all and if the liquor and food ran out, they only had to apply for more.

As more guests arrived and the liquor took effect, the noise below them increased until it became a bedlam. Guitars, accordions, a piano and singing, some melodious, some raucous in the extreme, added to the racket and extended right through the bar and into every room in the hotel.

Sadie and Jennie felt they were missing something in their quiet party and excusing themselves, made for the bar downstairs along with Leo. Sandy followed them on to the landing and had a look from the stairway. The place was packed to suffocation but the two young tarts and Leo, used to such an atmosphere, quite happily squeezed through the crowd milling around the beer and rum barrels in a haze of smoke and heat in the deafening uproar.

Reminds me of a Saturday night in a Glasgow pub, he thought. He returned to the peace of their room.

'The party seems to be a great success!' smiled Elmo.

'Well, it's off to a rousing start alright! Would you like to go down?'

'No thank you amigo,' replied Ramon, settled deep in a chair. 'We three can just stay here and enjoy a quiet drink. I have too much on my mind to enjoy a noisy party.'

'OK, but I'll leave you shortly. I daresay you two will have plenty to say to each other.'

Suddenly a shrill scream from below rent the air, followed by a high cackle of female laughter. The pandemonium hushed until only a few voices could be heard, crowned by the sonorous overtones of Teach's bass rumble.

Elmo jumped up. 'I'll bet that's a fight and I can guess who's in it,' she cried. 'I know that cackle! Come on! Let's have a look!'

She made for the stairway followed by the two men. Halting on the stairs some way down gave them a clear view over the crowd. It seemed a fight was indeed imminent. They all heard Teach announcing that he had no objection to the two girls having it out, short of murder, but Queensbury rules must be observed and both parties to agree to be searched in case either had a knife or a hat-pin.

A space rapidly appeared in the mêlée as the crowd cleared the floor for the combatants to engage with as much room as possible.

'I knew it,' cried Elmo, 'It's that black bitch Kate! Look! She's clawed Jennie!'

126

Through the smoke and haze, they could see Jennie getting first aid from her sister Sadie to some vivid scratches down one side of her face. At the other side of the 'ring' they could see Kate with a diabolical grin on her yellow face and rubbing her hands gleefully in readiness for the fray. She was being egged on by the mob excited by the palpable frisson of anticipation running through the room.

'Great Scot!' cried Sandy, sizing up the situation in some consternation. 'This can't go on! Where's Leo? Tell him to get the car. We've got to get Jennie out of this!'

'No use trying to interfere,' said Elmo. 'The crowd are in the mood for some fun and they'll have it! Look at Leo!'

Ever with an eye to business Leo was enthusiastically starting a 'book' and already accepting bets on the outcome of the contest. Catching sight of them on the stairs he pushed through the packed bodies to come up to them.

'Sah,' he said to Sandy, with a huge grin. 'You are about to witness your first fight between membahs of de profession. I will personally see that no murder is done. What about five dollars for your fancy?'

Sandy hastily declined. He sank down onto a stair tread feeling slightly nauseous.

The two girls were now circling like two cats, their fingers set in claw fashion, shoulders hunched and glaring for an opening. The spectators fell silent, mentally sizing up the odds. Bob leaned over the bar, grinning and offering five to one on Kate.

'I'll take you in ten dollar notes,' cried out Elmo and handed the money to Leo. Leo was soon back into the fray. The betting became fast and furious, the odds mainly in favour of Kate.

'What makes you so sure Jennie will be the victor?' asked Ramon.

'I've seen her fight before! She has a trick worth six of Kate's!'

Suddenly, with a combined yell, the two girls launched themselves at each other, clawing and scratching at faces and arms. After this furious onslaught and needing to catch their breath, as boxers lean to rest themselves, so did the girls, but by clutching each other's hair. Breathing heavily, they rocked backwards and forwards, only letting go when they had succeeded in pulling out a sufficient handful to stuff down their bosoms. After this restful occupation and with vigour renewed, the clawing and scratching started again, their faces suffused with rage and lips drawn back over their teeth; Kate's snarl having the edge on Jennie's for ferocity.

This exceedingly painful business went on between bouts of circling and glaring and hair-tearing, until both girls' faces showed streaks of blood where sharp nails had dug deep. The crowd were having the time of their lives, with moments of hushed suspense punctuated by roars of encouragement, and cheering and groaning with great gusto and theatrics.

'What's the idea of the souvenir bunches of hair?' asked Sandy revolted and yet feeling a raw excitement in the pit of his stomach.

'These women always do that,' said Ramon, his eyes on the two women. 'I've seen them in my own country. They show the total amount afterwards, as the Indian shows his scalps.'

'Good grief!' Sandy muttered, eyes compellingly riveted onto the two writhing girls.

Three times the young women fell in their strenuous efforts against each other, but each time their sister whores got them to their feet again, boosted by cheers and imprecations from the mob. Both were a dreadful spectacle, pouring with sweat and streaked with blood. Jennie's long tresses hung down damply over her face and back while Kate's hair stood out round her sallow face in a high frizz.

As they faced each other both panting and snarling, Kate suddenly reached out a long bony arm and, grabbing the front of Jennie's frock, ripped it down to the waist with one fierce gesture. A gasp went up. For a frail to have her breasts exposed in public was the worst insult.

'Jennie'll murder her!' whispered Elmo fiercely.

'In some circles it can only be avenged by death!' breathed Ramon.

Jennie, after the first initial shock, bared her teeth like a dog and screaming with rage, embedded her nails in Kate's scalp and hair. Then exerting all her strength, she administered the *coup de grâce*. She brought Kate's head sharply down towards the floor and at the same time brought her hard Scotch knee up with a bang on Kate's chin. There was a powerful and audible crack right on the point and Kate, the whites of her eyes showing as her eyes rolled up, collapsed flat on her back out for the count.

A terrific roar of applause greeted the victor, outdoing all the bedlam before. Meanwhile some sympathisers carried the inert Kate to a chair and started splashing her face with beer and trying to force some rum through her teeth.

Jennie stood clutching her torn garment to her half-naked body, grinning with delight and waving to the crowd. Sandy shouted over to Leo to pass her up the stairs and willing hands lifted the victorious trollop and passed her quickly over the heads of the cheering mob.

Sadie had worked her way back through the mob which was now headed, virtually *en masse*, toward the bar. She and Elmo got the exhausted girl to their room. They were busy tidying her up when Bob Teach strode into the room with a bottle of champagne in each hand.

'A drink for the winner and fifty dollars for Elmo, the lucky gel!' Leo followed him in and took the champagne in hand while Teach went back to the seething bar. Sandy, his stomach churning between the revulsion and excitement was glad of a draught of the fizz laced with brandy.

While Jennie rested from her labours on the bed, they settled down to a game of poker dice and rounds of drinks while the mob below resumed their racket and bellowed and roared afresh.

After a while Jennie sent Leo down to ask after her rival. Leo came back with the word that Kate was alright, but could she come up for a drink with Jennie. They all unanimously agreed and Leo went off again. A few moments later Kate walked in, somewhat shaky and pale, a round red button of flesh where she had received her knock-out, prominent on her damaged face.

Jennie got up, handed her late opponent a glass full of champagne and taking a cigarette from her own mouth put it between Kate's bleeding lips.

'No ill feelin's Kate?'

'No ill feelin's Jennie, but dat trick wid de knee is a new one on me. You must show me sometime to do 'im.'

'I already showed you Kate, doan you remembah?' Jennie grinned. Laughing uproariously, they settled down with the champagne and assorted reminiscences of past fights and slanging matches, with great animation and every sign of friendship.

Eventually tiring of the poker game, the others all lay about the room in various states of drunkenness. Jennie and Kate were on the bed flat out and singing 'Calypso Joe' while Elmo and Ramon lay in each other's arms on the sofa. Sandy sprawled in an armchair surrounded by bottles and acting as barman.

Leo meanwhile was adding to the uproar below with some of his pals, but he came back into the room to suggest they call it a night; the hour of the free fights had started and Bob's strong-arm men were getting busy ejecting the more obstreperous ones. They all agreed, except Kate who was very drunk, and said she'd stay, fights or no fights.

With some difficulty, they jostled their way through the hordes of booze hounds and out to the yard. When they got to the car, they had to pitch out a couple who obviously thought it a perfect place for some vigorous sex. That accomplished, Leo drove them back at a leisurely pace as if loth to go home and led them in singing maudlin and sentimental songs like '*Sweet Adeline*' and '*It was only a beautiful picture.*'

Sandy refused their pressing invitation to finish up at the Flag Hotel where he left them to continue their carouse. All he wanted now was his usual stroll alone in the early hours along the Careenage. He was by now very keen for its silence and serenity before turning in. That and a last cigar in peace.

❧ Chapter 14 ❧

After that night, Sandy's Scots Presbyterian soul was again in revolt. He resumed his courtship of Maureen and duly attended the round of tennis parties and supper dances and the occasional formal dinner to keep himself in evidence. He met many respectable girls and boys who behaved with perfect English propriety, enjoying life in a quiet way without ever seeking out the hot spots.

Maureen and her Granny hinted broadly, on more than one occasion, of the social and hygienic benefits of association with one's own colour. Sandy fairly inured to this prevalent point of view, deemed it best to seem to comply with what he privately considered as nonsense. He still had the longing to go where the fun was wild and free.

There were still occasions when Maur and he managed to elude the strict chaperonage of eagle-eyed Granny. He took these opportunities to embrace Maureen with a certain passion, which the sweet girl endured without protest and little response.

He tried hard to enjoy the straight and narrow, but having discovered the enticements of the low life, respectable Bajan life was dampening to his natural high spirits. Thankfully he still had his painting jaunts on Sundays with Boon to vary the monotony.

On one such morning, they'd selected a good view of the sea and coral reef and Sandy cast about for some shade to sit under. Settling down in the shade afforded by some thick foliage he was hailed by Boon.

'Hey Mac, I'd come out from under there if I were you, you could get a bad burn. That's Manchineel, poison bush.'

Scrambling out, he saw that it indeed held the pale yellow blooms and little green apples of the infamous

Manchineel. He found a safer spot on a rock and started to work his paint on the sized brown paper. The sight of those golden flowers unsettled his mind to the extent that he couldn't concentrate. His thoughts drifted to Elmo. Ramon had probably left by now on his date with danger or death. He must find Dunster and ask if there was news, or even go and ask Elmo herself. He felt restless and irritable.

'Heaven's man, it's all out of tone!' said Boon looking at his sketch with disgust. 'Look at that tree! It doesn't look as if it belongs in the background at all.'

Sandy regarded his efforts with a jaundiced eye and agreed, excusing himself by saying truthfully that he wasn't in the mood, so he'd better pack up; the day was getting too hot now for the paint anyway.

Getting his bike down to the road, he made off in the direction of the Beach Hotel in the hope of seeing the Golden Girl. It was early yet so the bar was deserted when he entered. He ordered an egg-nog from the bar-man.

To his surprise the swing half-doors opened and in strode the egregious Professor Goops. He was immaculately dressed in a spotless white drill suit, Panama hat and black and white American shoes and bearing down on Sandy in true Prussian military style. The sabre scars on his cheeks, relics from some mensur in the army, stood out on his closely shaven face.

'Have an egg-nogg, Herr Professor.' greeted Sandy

'*Danke schön, mein Schottlander! Donnerwetter*, you are just the man I wish to see!' he said gutturally, lapsing from his acquired Oxford accent, which he only did in moments of high tension.

Sandy was intrigued.

'Listen, your little friend Elmo is now alone. Corazon has just gone on that crazy, suicidal mission of his! I called on her last night and have got the invitation I wanted at last,' he growled, pale eyes even more protuberant than usual. 'The Obeah House! To see her perform! How would you like to come and see a little nature in the raw, eh? She says you know a Bajan called Leo who will be able to lead us to the place on the night she has selected for her séance.'

'I didn't know Leo was a student of Obeah,' said Sandy surprised, 'but I do know where to find him when needed.'

'*Sehr gut!* Do you want to come?'

'Yes, I would like to see what this manifestation stuff is all about, but I think I'd better ask Elmo if she minds me being a spectator first.' True, but he was looking for any excuse to see her. 'Where does all this Obeah business come from anyway?'

Goops launched himself into a veritable torrent about Voodoo, Ju-Ju, Egbo and a host of other demonology, animal cults and human sacrifices, ritual murder, demon possession and phallic worship and swept on to include secret societies and cabals. Before he had a chance to start on Christianity, Sandy decided it was time Goops was hauled off his hobby-horse and for himself to depart.

'Well, well, Professor. That's very interesting but if we are to see demons and phalluses and all that, the Obeah house ought to be highly diverting! I have to see a man about a dog now, so Goodbye Goops old chap.' And with that he hurriedly left the bar, promising to give Goops the required date after he had seen Elmo.

He cycled slowly up the Bay Road. The sun was now high overhead and blazed from a cloudless sky. A faint zephyr of breeze coming off the sea made the heat just tolerable and white dust rose lazily from the coral road and fell on the vibrant blooms of the bougainvillea and poinsettias that hung in bright curtains of colour over walls and hedgerows. A day for a cool shuttered room, cool drinks and the woman one loved, he thought with a sigh.

Coming to Elmo's white bungalow, he braked and looked for signs of life. It was closed, the jalousies shut. She was either asleep or out. Disappointed and restless, he set off for Hastings for the sweet soothing company of Aimée and Lois.

Entering the house, he found his erstwhile depressed friend, Jansen entertaining them in the lounge. Lois jumped up to get him a drink and Jansen came over and shook him warmly by the hand.

'Mac,' he said, 'by introducing me to these lovely people, you have saved my life - and my sanity for that matter!' He had certainly improved in appearance, looking fresh and immaculate and beaming happily. 'I come here every day and have a drink, but beer, not gin and I feel great!'

Sandy was delighted. Aimée looked blooming too he noticed.

'And I've gone doggone crazy over Aimée here, she's a grand girl. Why her voice just talkin' is like music!' and he bent his sentimental gaze on Aimée.

'Did you ever hear such rot!' she said lounging back in her Berbice chair, watching the smoke from her cigarette float lazily upwards. 'I can't get rid of him and now he wants to marry me Mac. But I refuse to live in that hell-hole Manàos.'

Lois came in with Sandy's iced beer.

'And what's to become of me pray, when you marry Karl?' she asked

'Well,' said Karl, 'You can marry Mac here!'

'Great idea,' Lois replied, 'when he's already mad on two women.'

'Two? Who are these two women?' asked Sandy innocently, refreshing himself from his cold beer.

'Maureen Dare and Elmo Crofts, only you can't make up your mind which one has the most appeal to you.'

'Wrong Lois, there are three of you. You, Maureen and Elmo, and you all have a different appeal. The point is, none of the three is mad on me, so there it is.'

Lois sat down close beside Sandy on the settee and seized his hand in a warm clasp. Karl had turned to Aimée and was telling her that he was giving up the old tramp steamer and would get a ship from a more civilized port, maybe in California, he said.

'Let's leave them to it,' said Lois, still holding on to Sandy's hand. She led him out to the verandah. 'You'll stay to lunch won't you dear?'

'Sure darling. Let's relax on this for a while,' he replied heading for a large hammock strung across the end of the verandah. They settled into it enjoying the feel of their bodies against one another. As they lay comfortably in each other's arms, the sun falling across them was making them very warm.

'Let's get into our swimsuits darling, this sun's a bit hot for all these clothes.'

'Good idea. We'll be having a swim before lunch in any case,' said Lois.

'I love the delightful lack of conventions in this house, darling and being able to lunch in our beach robes after our swim. It is so nice to be free of all the palaver of dressing again for it,' he said, helping Lois out of the hammock.

They settled down more comfortably in their costumes in the hammock again.

'Sandy,' said Lois after a while, 'Aimée says, you'll have to marry me if you give me a baby.'

Sandy nearly fell out of the hammock.

'Great Scot! What have you told her?' he cried, horrified.

'You great silly,' she said, 'I always tell her everything, that's why we're such pals.' Lois lay back on Sandy's arm, nibbling at the petals of a flower she'd picked from the foliage hanging nearby. Her heavy lids and thick lowered lashes hid her eyes but Sandy detected a slight smirk at the corner of her mouth.'

Sandy was annoyed. He withdrew his arm and sat up with his back to her, his thoughts jumping all over the place.

'Thanks for the warning Lois. I don't feel like pursuing a love affair when every movement is recorded and repeated to a third party.'

'Don't be so childish, Sandy,' she chided. 'I never gave her the slightest detail. I only answered a direct question, that's all.'

'And what was that?'

'Well, if you must know, after Karl had gone that night - he left soon after you - Aimée was brushing her hair at the dressing table, and she suddenly turned to me and said, 'Did Sandy seduce you darling?'

'What, just like that?'

'Yes, just like that.'

'Crumbs! She's got a nerve! What did you say?'

'I can assure you, I was a bit taken aback, although I shouldn't have been surprised; I am used to Auntie not being one to beat about the bush, - so I just stammered something.'

'So,' she said. 'You are very silly to give in so soon but tell him that if there are any babies he'll have to marry you.' That's all dear.' She didn't say any more, just went on brushing her hair, and truly Sandy, she hasn't made a single reference to it again.'

Somewhat mollified, he turned back and took her in his arms again.

'Don't worry darling, there won't be any babies and if there are, of course I'll marry you!' thinking with some misgiving of his dear mama's welcome at his turning up with a half-caste bride, however beautiful, and infant to boot. He took mental refuge in the Bank's policy that junior employees couldn't marry and gave it a silent cheer.

With time on their hands to enjoy, the four of them spent the day eating and drinking, dozing or swimming, or paired off making love in secluded corners of the beach or house.

To Sandy it was a blissful, dissolute way to spend a Sunday; so utterly different from the strict Sabbatarian routine of Scotland he was accustomed to all his life. The morning church, the heavy mid-day meal prepared the night before; minimal cooking only being allowed, the mooning about in the afternoon afraid to whistle, play, play the piano or sing, all strictly forbidden by the church, and then high tea and church again at night. No small wonder that with liberty at last, under the lure of this untrammelled way of life, he took to all the pleasurable delights at hand. To him this was paradise on earth.

When darkness fell, he and Lois were lying together on a settee in companionable silence in the darkness of the lounge, while Aimée and her new friend were out on the verandah. Sandy found himself thinking over his encounter that morning with Goops and his extraordinary conversation. He felt a renewed desire to see Elmo, but lacked the moral courage to tell Lois that he intended to see her that night, if he could find her.

'You won't mind if I go early, will you darling?' he began.

'What's the hurry, 'she interjected. 'Are you tired of my company?' she added petulantly, turning in his arms.

'Now Lois, none of that. I'm merely tired, that's all, and I feel like turning in early,' he answered, trying to keep his voice even and reassuring. 'We've had a lovely time together all day after all.'

'You never leave so early as a rule,' she said, in no way mollified. 'Are you sure you haven't got a date with another girl?' she added, a note of rising suspicion in her voice. Sandy lay silent.

'Right,' he burst out, 'You've asked for it now! No. Not a date, but I want to see Elmo about something private.'

Lois threw herself off the settee onto the floor shrieking and kicking, then drumming her heels fiercely on the rug. Sandy gawped at her in utter astonishment and rising impatience as Aimée rushed in, switching on the light to see what the hullabaloo was all about. She was closely followed by Karl.

'Mac, what on earth has happened?' she cried and fell to her knees beside the hysterical Lois, shaking and slapping the poor girl. 'She's in hysterics. What have you been doing to her?'

'Nothing Aimée, I just told her I was going to see Elmo.'

'Goodness, that's enough! That was cruel. You know how she cares for you!'

Sandy stood there feeling foolish and uncomfortable. Jansen looked at him with a grin as if he knew fine what was going through his mind. For want of something to do, Sandy poured out a glass of water and handed it to Aimée; as if that would do any good, he thought, unless she throws it over Lois. Aimée's ministrations however, were beginning to bear fruit and Lois was coming back to normal.

Relieved, he thought, - now or never!

'I can't stand this kind of silly behaviour' he said loudly and made a cowardly dash for the door and his bicycle. Leaping on it, he pedalled furiously along the road as if the fiends were after him, but seeing a light on in Elmo's bungalow, slowed down, braked and flung his bike onto the grass outside.

He dashed into the living room. Both women were sitting amusing themselves, Elmo working on something at the table and Leila lounging with a novel.

'Hello Mac,' she said looking up from her tattered copy of 'Three Weeks.' 'Someone chase you? You look *un peu distrait.*'

Elmo laughed. 'Really Mac, who's been mussing up your hair and why the agitation? Lois been too much for you?'

'What are you talking about?' he said running a hand through his hair to tidy it.

'You need a drink. Educated guess dear. Don't blush. Don't forget she is a lady of colour and understands passion, in spite of her swanky airs.'

'You know too much Elmo,' he said aggrievedly. 'Yes, she cut up rough when I mentioned you.'

'I'm flattered! Leila, get the poor lad a drink, - some beer off the ice, and also some of that flying fish and salad will do.

Leila sighed and put down her book, but she headed obediently for the kitchen.

'What have you got there?' he asked going over to her where she continued to work at something in her hands. 'Looks like something familiar.'

'Have a look,' said the girl and held out a plasticine model to him.

It was a well-executed coloured figurine of a stout gentleman with a dark red face, a black sombrero and bell-bottomed trousers.

'Nice work. Whose portrait?'

'That devil, Gomez,' she replied with a hiss. 'When I finish him, I'm going to put a nice sharp needle through his black heart with a few words of Obeah. That'll kill him alright.'

'I thought I recognised the kind of figure,' said Sandy, 'they do that kind of thing in the Highlands in my own country, but I never heard of it doing much good, or harm for that matter.'

'That's because they didn't know the right words to say by one who is truly chosen,' she said, laying the figure aside for future execution. 'Have you heard from old man Goops?' she asked.

140

'Yes, that's why I'm here. He says you have invited us to the Obeah House next time you go there, but why invite that old buzzard?'

'He knows plenty about Black Magic, but he says that prophesy is bunk. I'm going to show him that I, as a fetish woman, can prophesy. He thinks I'm a hysteric and a fake. I'll show him something that will surprise him.'

She turned her golden gaze on him. 'I want you to be there Mac, to tell me what I say. I'm not conscious you know when the Loi enters me, and people won't always tell me what I say. I want to find out how Ramon is to get on - if he is to succeed or die.'

'I don't like the idea of this at all Elmo. If we find he is to die, I don't want to be the one to break your heart!'

'There will be no heartbreak. I only want to know what the future holds for me. It rests with him. Am I to live a worthwhile life in the sun, or live it and then perish only in darkness?' She spoke softly with such sadness. Sandy's heart swelled with sorrow for this young and lovely creature, condemned by her grotesque upbringing in the dark arts to its evil and black superstitions.

With a soft resigned sigh, she turned to the figurine of Gomez. She looked at it calculatingly for a moment, then taking out a needle from her work-basket, picked him up and slowly pierced the clay in the region of the heart.

'There!' she hissed. 'mourir, aba, abaha, hain, hain, die, Gomez die! Let the bullet pierce your yellow heart!' She laid the figure down on the table with the needle stuck in it.

'Doesn't sound very convincing Mac, does it?' she said with a wry smile. 'As a fetish woman *I* give the words power. She dropped her voice. 'Here's Leila, now don't fail me. Two days' time probably. Leo will take you to the place,' she murmured, as Leila entered with the food and drinks. The mood was broken.

~ *Chapter 15* ~

The following evening, Sandy cornered the Professor just finishing his meal out at Stafford House.

'It's all set Professor. Should be in a day or so.'

'*Ganz gut!*' he said, pushing back his plate. 'Credo in diabolum'. Now we will prove whether the Haitian is a real fetish woman or a fake! As you know I have made a very close study of pagan worship and native religions. I have witnessed the Leopard cult in West Africa, Voodoo in Haiti, Nimm in Liberia and a host of other sects all over the world, so I will not be fooled. I think Elmo has ability and is well-versed in Obeah, but I doubt if she is a true fetish woman!' He gave a short guttural laugh. 'I think she is a plain sexual hysteric influenced by the fact that she has Haitian ancestry. I put her manifestations down to some psychical disturbance preceding her menstrual period. However,' he shrugged eloquently, 'we shall see.'

'Well, that would be the trend of your thinking Goops old man. The rank evil is in all this diabolical superstitious stuff manipulating a young and innocent girl and tainting her mind, damn it all, - since her childhood! It's nothing short of criminal. But I can't bear the thought that she *is* possessed of some devil or Loi, or whatever the deuce it is. If it is true then I imagine there would be little hope but a ghastly gradual mental and physical degeneration in store for her.' Sandy felt chilled at the thought. 'Perhaps she should get some sort of medical help,' he added reflectively, then collected his wits before Goops could get into his stride again. 'Well, *Auf weidersehn*, Professor, I'll let you know as soon as I get the tip from Leo.' and beat a hasty retreat.

As Elmo had foreseen, Leo got word to him two days later, that the time had come. He would meet them at Bob Teach's Select Bar at 9pm to take them to Black Rock.

Thinking it befitted the solemn occasion, Sandy dressed in a dark lounge suit and set off to walk to the Select. Arriving at Teach's a little before the appointed time he saw that Leo had already arrived, as a ragged black youth was on guard over Leo's sports car.

He went in and found Leo and the professor at the bar, so he joined them and fortified himself with a large scotch and soda. Goops was looking very academic in a dark suit and Four-in-Hand tie while Leo sported a black jacket, striped trousers and patent shoes, putting Sandy in mind of a West African graduate of Balliol he knew. For a minute he felt as if they were all about to attend a funeral and said so.

'If there is one, I hope that it won't be ours. Whites don't normally attend Obeah functions,' commented Goops lugubriously. Leo calmed his fears by saying that as the High Priestess herself had invited them, not to worry, their persons were untouchable.

Finishing their drinks, they made for the car. Leo let in the clutch and with a roar of exhaust, they set off along the coast road to Black Rock. When they reached the crowded native village Sandy rather wished they'd taken a buggy as being a lot less conspicuous, for the car was immediately besieged by dozens of Negroes of both sexes all eager to examine the automobile, the like of which they had never seen.

Leo scattered the admiring and voluble crowd with sundry cursings, headlights blazing and the klaxon blaring a tremendous sustained blast.

Soon they were through the built-up area and making for the sugar plantations. After being somewhat jolted along a mile of narrow rough road, they reached a clearing in front of a small wood. Elmo's empty buggy, minus its fur rug was there, so they pulled up beside it. The only other vehicle was an antiquated relic, from about the 1860's Sandy guessed. It had high clumsy wheels and the body was slung on thick leather straps.

'Who on earth belongs to that?' he asked Leo.

'You doan know whose carriage dat be?' he said in some surprise.

'Haven't the faintest.'

'In dat case sah, I say no moah. Mebbe you find out later, but I doan want to make trouble fo' no one.' After this provocatively enigmatic remark he switched off the engine and lights and taking a hurricane lamp from the car, lit it and told the other two to follow him on foot into a belt of trees.

They went into the wood and saw, moving through the trees the twinkling of moving lanterns and heard the chatter of native voices, some speaking in French. They followed and then Leo halted at the edge of another clearing. They had arrived at the Obeah House.

This was a wooden erection of no discernible beauty. It was like a large barn. It was raised off the ground on iron rails and was reached by a short flight of steps. The scene was lit by hurricane lamps being carried by several of the men in this largely male gathering. The figure of a heavily-veiled woman in black was standing aside talking to a Negro with grey hair who reminded Sandy strongly of Beresford, the head waiter at the Sabana Club.

The door of the house stood open and Leo led them up the steps to enter the building. A strong odour of incense pervaded the air from two burners on tripods at the far end of the room. The place was crowded already, by people sitting cross-legged and forming three sides of a square facing the end wall. The centre was left vacant.

In the centre at the end of the room there was a rude form of altar on which lay a short naked sword and a human skull. This was flanked by the *piéce de resistance*, as far as

Sandy was concerned. Two colossal figures, each about 15 feet high, of a naked female and naked male. They were seated with the feet and posteriors on the floor. The huge figures being unclothed and in this position, their genitals were in full view and grossly enlarged. These had been painted with red enamel and the male's phallus stuck up like a club. Goops did promise him phalluses after all, but he rather thought this specimen was fully adequate in the singular.

Those Negroes seated around the edge of the central space all had drums. Leo pointed out three important ceremonial drums called respectively, Mama, Papa and Boula. An official in a garment like a red night-shirt, led them to their appointed places. Sandy was glad to note that it was by the open door as the pungent smell of unwashed humanity and incense didn't combine to advantage.

'What about all the people outside?' he asked Leo, intrigued at the numbers drawn to the place.

'There'll be room for a few more, but de rest will have to be satisfied wid squattin' and lookin' through de open door.'

Despite the fact that his and Goops were the only white faces he could see, nobody seemed to take much notice of them for which Sandy was heartily glad. He could only assume that this was due to Elmo's dictum as High Priestess and that the tom-toms had passed the word.

Behind the altar, he now noticed two curtains of some black material ornamented with tinsel stars, drawn across to meet in the centre. They moved occasionally as if there was someone behind them. A young black girl in an abbreviated red silk frock, came out of one side of the curtain. She was carrying a lighted taper with which she lit the wicks that floated in oil in various vessels about the room.

The idle drums now started their rhythmic beat, the supple fingers of the Negroes rapidly striking the stretched skin of their instruments, their dark hands flickering almost hypnotically in the lamplight. The three ceremonial drums had the loudest call while the rest kept up a kind of chorus. Sandy watched the expressions on the faces of the drummers as they became absorbed in their rhythms, rhythms that could stir in the African breast the sexual senses to the point of frenzy, soften the senses to dire melancholy, or raise them to transports of rage and defiance.

The hurricane lights were extinguished and passed outside. The half-gloom of the room, the pervasive smell, the throbbing of the drums and the dark shining faces lit only by flickering oil wicks gave a sense of foreboding and mystery. The centre of the room was still empty and Sandy wondered what was to be enacted there. The two colossi had oil-lamps of their own placed between their massive feet and illuminating their red enamelled genitals. Then Goops broke the spell by muttering that the whole thing looked like freemasonry to him. This made Sandy giggle, especially when Goops added that the two figures were the native idea of the pillars of King Solomon's Temple.

Leo was seated behind Sandy and bent forward to whisper the advice that if drinks or cigarettes were passed round, the drinks were alright but the fags would probably be marihuana and no good for him, so it would be better to smoke his own.

Temporarily distracted from the main scene by Leo's whispered advice, he then became aware that his other neighbour was the heavily veiled woman he'd seen outside. She seemed to have a familiar perfume about her, certainly not a native's. Something from the Rue de la Paix in Paris.

'Goops,' he whispered, 'the lady on my left; do you know who it is?'

The professor was ever a realist and never wasted any time in dealing in mysteries.

'Mrs Dare, I should think,' he muttered back without even looking.

'Christopher!' he exclaimed.

'Don't be surprised at anything you see at Black Rock,' said the voice of Mrs Dare. She raised her veil and smiled at Sandy with her cynical smile.

Before he'd had a chance to absorb this surprise, a terrific crash from a hidden gong made Sandy jump and with this dramatic signal, the curtains parted and a tall male figure entered clad in a red robe that reached to his naked feet with a wide blue sash around it.

'Good Lord! Whatever next!' exclaimed Sandy in more astonishment. There stood Beresford, the head waiter from the Sabana Club in Bridgetown, all trace of obsequiousness gone. In its place, an air of arrogance and command. He came centre stage.

In a deep bass voice of uncommon power, he commenced a chant that was then taken up and repeated by the assembled Negroes. Even Mrs Dare joined in with her contralto.

'How do you know this stuff?' whispered Sandy.

'I ought to,' she answered. 'I've been attending these cults since I was a child in Haiti.'

The drumming and the chanting took on a frenzied note. Beresford moved to one side where a hideously-carved stool had been placed for him. He seated himself with great dignity.

'What in goodness name is Beresford supposed to be?' he asked Leo.

'He's a Papaloi, a priest of Obeah. A witch doctor. He sometimes prophesies too.'

The idea of the Club's head waiter performing as a jungle wizard, thought Sandy, certainly bore out Mrs Dare's exhortation about finding no surprises at Black Rock. The singing ceased and about a dozen black girls entered from the curtains and passed on either side of the altar to take up positions in the centre of the floor space.

They wore a short kirtle of red material edged with blue silk fringing. The rhythm of the drums changed and quickened as the girls commenced to writhe and stomp, their torsos and limbs twisting to the beat and firm young buttocks clashing together at intervals in a wild dance. Many of the movements were highly suggestive and many a kirtle flew up to their waists, as often as not exposing considerable smooth bare flesh. The enthusiasm on the faces of the male spectators put Sandy in mind of Tam o' Shanter peering through the window at Alloway Kirk at the young witch in her 'cutty sark.' Goops was grinning all over his ugly mug and Mrs Dare seemed to have lost all interest in the proceedings and was smoking a cigarette with a heavy odour he took to be marihuana and looking at the floor. Sandy was just getting hot and bored.

'I want to see Elmo, Leo' he hissed 'not a jungle congo.'

'Won't be long now, Mistah Mac. Mr Beresford, he cut dis ceremony short for yo' benefit. He doan want yo to know too much anyway,' he whispered, grinning. 'Wait, I get yo' a drink.'

He disappeared and returned shortly with some glasses and a bottle of rum. Sandy and Goops had a good shot of the stuff, which Sandy remarked was unusually palatable.

'Yessah. Fifty year old; a present from Mr Beresford fo' his guests.'

Courtesy of the Club's cellars no doubt, thought Sandy. Mrs Dare didn't pass up the chance of some booze and helped herself as well.

After a final high leap and a crashing together of those young buttocks as they met in mid-air, the girls all disappeared behind the curtain. At once about two dozen of the younger male spectators got up and made for the door.

'Where are they off to?' asked Sandy.

The Prof and Mrs Dare both laughed.

148

'Same place as the guests of the Roman Emperors went after dinner; into the woods perchance to find a nymph. Nero of course, already had them waiting there,' rumbled Goops with a grin.

Just then Beresford stood up and set up another chant.

'Kala kasesa Elmo. Kala Kasesa Elmo.' his deep voice intoned as the drums softened their throbbing and then suddenly, they boomed out in a thundering crescendo. The black tinsel-starred curtains parted and the vision he'd been waiting for appeared. The Golden Girl herself. She stood for a moment with arms upstretched, holding the curtains apart, slender body poised, with her head thrown back.

She leaped over the altar to the middle of the floor to roars of approval from the spectators for their High Priestess. Sandy cheered like a fool. She paused for a moment in her white silk frock fringed with gold beads, the hem barely at mid-thigh, her slim waist encircled by a gold chain of curious design. The golden flowers of the Manchineel were entwined in her chestnut hair, which hung in clustering ringlets about her face and fell past her shoulders down to her waist.

To the music of the drums, the lovely creature danced, weaved and pirouetted on her arched feet with the toenails shining with mother of pearl and her pale gold shapely legs gleaming in the lamp-light.

Gradually her dancing became more exaggerated and her pirouettes changed in intensity, her long flower-strewn hair streaming around her. The drums increased their tempo with her, her twisting and whirling growing ever more rapid and frequent.

'She's working herself up to a climax,' growled Goops obviously enjoying the spectacle, with his head stuck forward and watching her like a snake watching its prey.

Look at the ugly old devil, thought Sandy, feeling slightly nauseated by his avidity. He's revelling in all this untamed jungle stuff.

The Negro spectators, including the drummers, followed her every movement with gleaming eyes. Even Mrs Dare looked fascinated. She sat, her burning orbs with pupils dilated, fixed on the swiftly moving figure. Sandy's eyes sought Elmo's face.

As her whirling grew ever faster, he watched in some alarm a change coming over her features. Her head extended ever more backward, the rosy lips became paler and receded more and more from her teeth and sweat gleamed wetly on her cheeks. Her beauty was distorting into a veritable mask of ugliness and evil in a grotesque parody of her features. In that moment, Sandy found no difficulty in believing that the soul of the girl was indeed fleeing and the 'Mystere' was entering to take charge of her body.

Tense with apprehension and almost holding his breath, Sandy watched her with straining eyes. Beresford got up and silently and rapidly extinguished all the wicks except those by the colossi. The girl flitted noiselessly about the floor in the semi-darkness, the drums now only a muted roll. She was now partly under the influence of the priest who, with light movements of his hands enticed her nearer the altar. He thrust his hand through the curtains and it came out grasping a struggling and squawking bird; a white cockerel. He quickly handed it to the girl who grasped it by the neck and with one swift movement seized the sword from the altar and in a flash beheaded it. Blood spurted from its severed neck. The drums thundered, the Negroes shouted and chanted while Elmo continued her frenzied dance, her gyrations and writhing splattering them with blood and feathers.

'Goops! This is bloody awful! Let's get out,' hissed Sandy repelled.

'Not a bit,' retorted Goops, not taking his eyes off the scene for an instant. 'This is the eternal ritual cleansing by blood and sacrifice,' he growled. 'The priesthood has always wallowed in blood, even your evangelists with their blood-thirsty hymns!'

Sandy felt sick and was glad of a hefty glass of the rum that Leo quickly handed him. Worse was to come. Throwing the still convulsing bird from her onto the altar, she whirled and turned to the centre of the floor and stood rigidly, legs apart. Then a cry, a soaring sound of fear and despair issued from her parted lips. Her hands stretched down to the edge of her silk garment and with a violent gesture, ripped it from hem to throat, baring her golden body in the flickering light, with the coiled snake tattoo showing dark on her breast. The force had snapped the golden girdle at her waist, which flew into the shadows. Casting the riven dress from her, she seemed like one possessed. Her dancing became convulsive, frenzied and to Sandy's horror, she appeared to be having an epileptic fit. Her body was shining with sweat and the Negroes were being wrought up to a dangerous tension, gasps and hissing sounds issuing from their throats and hands stretched out as if to grasp the moving figure.

Sandy's throat was dry, his nerves at fever pitch. He was in terror lest Elmo's body be physically profaned. The tension in him was almost unbearable as he held himself in readiness with some crazy idea of rushing to her aid.

'I was wrong!' muttered Goops gutturally. 'She is now fully possessed by the Loi. She *is* a true fetish woman!'

He'd hardly finished speaking when the body stilled, seemingly no longer inhabited by Elmo Crofts but possessed by the Loi, for a deep baritone voice issued from her throat as the drums ceased. The feeble glimmer from the oil lamps was behind her so did not wholly reveal her nakedness but flung a double V of shadow from her body to the floor. Immediately behind her stood Beresford, standing before the altar, his tall figure made gigantic by the strong shadows. His hands moved rhythmically in the long wide sleeves.

He's got her hypnotised, thought Sandy angrily, swallowing more rum to ease his acute tension and dry throat.

At first the words were an unintelligible mix of Creole French and seemingly Haitian dialect, but gradually the deep voice spoke clearly in English. The words tumbled out incoherently, the baritone voice speaking of grim forebodings, of the death and suffering of the races of the world. Goops reacted strongly to the prophecies and sat up expectantly when Germany and the Kaiser were mentioned as if waiting for triumphant tidings. If he was, he was doomed to disappointment as the voice spoke of defeat and humiliation for Deutschland. Sandy, under the soothing influence of the 50-year-old rum, was now moving into a state of improbability and he felt sure Beresford was feeding her stuff he'd picked up at the club and that Elmo was just raving.

Then Elmo's expression altered and the evil mask changed to terror, and tears streamed from her heavy half-closed eyes. Her voice resumed its normal timbre as she cried out in heart-rending tones,

'Ramon! Ramon! -don't go up the steps! don't - don't enter the building! Can't you see? He's waiting for you! - Stop! - Stop! - He's going to fire!'

Her voice rose in a crescendo of fear ending on a wild shriek, and with her arms outstretched, she fell headlong forward onto the floor. Her prostrate form trembled a moment then stilled.

Sandy froze, appalled. An excited chattering broke out among the puzzled spectators, who didn't understand the sudden change and Elmo's own voice and beseeching words. Beresford immediately re-appeared from the shadows carrying her fur robe, which he rapidly cast over her. Gently he raised her and with great dignity, carried the unconscious body of the girl around the altar and through the parted curtains which were pulled to behind them.

With one accord Sandy and Goops got up and made their way through the crush to the door. Sandy couldn't wait to get into the fresh air, anxious and horrified for Elmo. As they came down the steps, Leo was waiting for them with the lantern. The Negroes were filing out of the door talking volubly about Elmo's prophecies and her talk of war as they re-lit their lanterns and moved towards the trees.

Following Leo's recommendation, the trio trooped through the little wood with the chattering crowd towards the vehicles parked in the clearing. Sandy saw Mrs Dare getting into the ancient carriage and being followed by someone who looked suspiciously like Thunder and Lightning.

Goops and Sandy walked over to the car as the milling crowd gradually disappeared into the night. They left a silence so profound it was as if they had not been there at all. The change was remarkable and gave a strange air of unreality to the place. Sandy and Goops stood still, caught for a moment in the silence.

Then just as they were debating their next move with Leo, they saw Beresford crossing the clearing, who having donned his usual dark suit, and his obsequious manner with it, came over to them.

'Elmo would like to see you alone Mr MacNeil.'

'Is she alright after her ordeal?' he asked, somewhat surprised.

'Perfectly, sir, I think you will find she shows no sign of distress or anxiety.'

'You go along,' said Goops with his guttural laugh. 'I'll get Leo to drive me down to the village where I can study the natives after a night with Obeah. I'll give you a couple of hours and wake you up with a toot on the horn.' He gave Sandy a lewd wink and jumped into the car, and with Leo at the wheel, they sped away in a cloud of exhaust and dust.

Sandy gladly followed Beresford back through the trees and around to the back of the Obeah House, quite anxious to see for himself how Elmo had come through the frenzy he had witnessed. Beresford, still in the rôle of Club servant, showed him into a room and discretely vanished.

He entered in some trepidation. Elmo lay on a divan in a diaphanous green frock, smiling and looking as beautiful as ever.

'Hello darling,' she greeted him. 'You look scared! Every time you come to see me you look frightened of something. What's the matter?'

'I expected to see you a wreck. Pale and haggard and so forth,' he replied relieved to see her back to normal and no signs of collapse.

'Sit down here and relax,' she said, making room for him on the divan.

'Is this the Mamaloi's Holy of Holies?' he asked sitting beside her and looking around him at the exotic room. A large bowl of Elmo's favourite Manchineel flowers glowed on a table. The walls and ceilings were painted with grotesque figures while the furniture, in some dark wood, was carved with the semblance of animals, reptiles and birds. He felt sure that Elmo had added her own feminine touch with the attractive cushions and fabrics. They were of material that was of native make, with native designs and colours. The large mat on the floor was obviously of native manufacture and a leopard skin rug lay by the side of the divan.

'Yes.' she said flicking a drum by the couch. It emitted a surprisingly loud boom that made Sandy jump, his nerves still exacerbated by the night's performance. The drum was about three feet high and was of a zebra skin stretched tightly over some large hollow gourd and very artistically made.

'It's Zulu,' she said, 'a charming fellow brought it from South Africa for me.' A black girl entered.

'Bring me a jug of iced beer and limes and two glasses. You'll have a drink Sandy?'

'Yes, a nice cold beer sounds just what the doctor ordered!'

The girl departed on her errand.

'How do you feel after that frightful performance Elmo?'

'I feel fine. I don't remember anything about it. I never do. *Was* it so frightful?' she asked. 'I'm sorry I stripped off my frock. I don't do that as a rule, not since I was a child at school. Something must have upset me tonight, something unusual. Are you cross with me?'

'Not now that I know you're not in the habit of running around the Obeah House in the nude. I must admit it gave me a bit of a shock!'

The girl brought in the beer, limes and glasses and set them down on a small table near them. As she made to withdraw, Elmo warned her not to return unless drummed for.

Sandy and Elmo drank their lime flavoured iced beer and Elmo turned down the oil-lamp till it was a mere glimmer. She pulled Sandy gently down beside her,

'Beresford said I foretold a great war, but that was all he told me. I think he was withholding something from me darling, otherwise how would I have got into such a state? When I came to, my eyes and face were wet and I felt exhausted. I recovered alright after I'd had a cold sponge down and some kola nut, but something else happened, I'm sure. Did I get through to Ramon?'

'Yes, you told him not to mount some steps and not to enter some building, that's all,' replied Sandy, a prey to mixed emotions but instinctively feeling unable to tell her about the warning about someone waiting and about to fire at Ramon. For one thing he could not bring himself to distress her anew after such an emotional ordeal, especially since she had no memory of it. It was much better that she hadn't, he felt. She seemed so relaxed and normal after it all now, he didn't relish the idea of that changing; he'd had

155

enough high drama for one night. He much preferred this sweet mood of loving intimacy, and anyway, he didn't want her mind to be on Ramon and his plight now that he had her in all her exotic gorgeousness to himself at long last.

'Thanks darling. I'll cable a warning to him tomorrow that he will understand perhaps. But I fear for him Sandy, I fear for him!' she whispered.

Sandy put his arms around her. 'You must love him a great deal Elmo.'

'No, 'she sighed, 'I don't love him, but I like him very much and he is my only means of escape from a very unpleasant mode of living. He knows all about me and is willing to condone what has happened in my past, which shows what a good man he is.'

She cuddled into the comfort of Sandy's arms and the warmth of his body.

They lay silent for a while. The proximity and perfume from Elmo's desirable body stirred Sandy's senses anew. The terrifying excitement of the night's events had heightened them already but now they were assailed by Elmo's gentle endearments and caresses and soft kisses. Once more Sandy felt himself drowning in an intoxicating surge of physical and emotional arousal. The sensuality of the room, the glimmering light, all added to the stripping away of any reservations Sandy had. The sheer joy and delight in her presence and being the object of the absorbed interest of the glorious woman in his arms, her tantalizing kisses and caresses, his own longing and desire for her for so long, swept all other thoughts away. The blood, the frenzy, the devil-possession were forgotten. Everyone and everything else were blotted from his mind. She was here, his for the asking, eager, responsive, passionate. The longing and need to be part of that beautiful flesh, this most fascinating of young women, filled his mind and dissolved his will to that one purpose.

It was almost a kind of agony to move away from her sufficiently to divest himself of his clothes but his senses were amply rewarded as he did so by seeing Elmo's lovely form emerging from the diaphanous folds of her only garment. He could barely wait to enter and possess that smooth golden body at last.

※

Several resounding blasts from Leo's klaxon penetrated the still night. Elmo roused Sandy from sleep. He jumped up, feeling for his clothes in the semi-gloom. Elmo sat up and turned up the lamp. She looked so sweet and lovely in the mist of palest green that billowed around her as she watched him hurriedly dress and smooth his hair. Just seeing her like that was sufficient to arouse him again. She smiled at seeing the awakening passion in his eyes and body.

'They are waiting Sandy. You must go.'

'Yes, I know I must. Oh, what a gorgeous thing it is to love you, Elmo. I must see you again soon.'

'No not soon, darling. Kiss me Goodbye.'

'Goodbye? Why, where are you going?'

'Oh, Caracas perhaps. Who knows? *Quien sabe.*'

Sandy didn't take her seriously but left her regretfully all the same with a last embrace.

Leo was waiting outside with the hurricane lamp, face and teeth gleaming in its radiance. They made their way through the trees. He found Goops sitting back in the car, a large cigar between his teeth.

'*Vorwaerts,* Leo!' he shouted, breathing rum all over Sandy as he got in and sat down beside him. 'Forward with this chaste Hypolytus who has been resisting his Phaedra! To Bridgetown, Charioteer!'

'Goops, you're drunk!'

'*Jawohl, mein Schottlander! Ist gut, ja?*'

ᵈ Chapter 16 ᵈ

A few nights later out at the Stafford Hotel where Sandy was having dinner, Dunster came in and espying Sandy, crossed to his table.

'Hey Mac. Heard the news about Corazon? Not good, old man, not good.'

He flung himself into a chair. 'Damn bloody bad, actually,' he added looking more than usually lugubrious. 'He got himself into the Dictator's Palace alright by some kind of subterfuge and armed with a revolver, but he only got as far as the entrance hall and one of Gomez' security guards recognised him and shot the poor fool dead.'

'Good God, Thunder!' ejaculated Sandy, vividly and horribly conscious of Elmo's exactly prophetic words. He was seized with a sudden surge of guilt for withholding the full extent of Elmo's warning from her.

'Apparently the policeman was quicker on the draw than Corazon. There was an abortive attempt by his pals to seize Caracas, but once news of Corazon's death spread, - well, without his leadership the attempted revolution was doomed to failure. Gomez still rules Venezuela and is likely to die with his boots on. He may have the emotions of a stallion at stud, but he has the Yank financiers by the short hairs and his country is secure from a monetary point of view.'

'What about Elmo, do you know she had a premonition of his death?'

'Yes, Mrs Dare told me. She acted as stooge for me at your precious séance out at Black Rock. If you read my paper, you would have seen that I too predicted the failure of de Castro's coup.'

'If Elmo read it, she would deduce you got it from Mrs Dare. Mind she doesn't put a fetish on you!'

'Tripe! Cassandra don't frighten me! Her prophesies are the result of her sub-conscious thoughts and when she has a fit, or auto-hypnotism or whatever it is, out come the prognostications!'

'I love your cynicism Dunst! Or is that supposed to be a learned diagnosis?' asked Sandy with some sarcasm. Thunder snorted derisively.

'If you've finished that revolting fish dish, I'll join you for the meat course. I'm really only in the mood for something alcoholic, but I don't want to offend dear Miss Weir's sensibilities any more than I can help.'

They ate in morose silence. Sandy was genuinely sorry about Corazon. He'd really liked and admired the man. What a waste, he thought, not relishing his food and a prey to mixed feelings.

After they'd eaten, they sat over coffee looking out towards the Savannah, talking desultorily of the failed coup. Sandy saddened, but also somewhat conscience-stricken, consoled himself by some certainty that even with the full warning, nothing would have stopped Ramon from his attempt at Gomez. Would he have believed Elmo, fired as he was by his patriotic zeal? Sandy pushed the unanswerable question away. He looked instead at Thunder slumped untidily in his chair and gazing moodily ahead. If possible, he was looking paler and more haggard than ever. His dank black hair stuck to his scalp in thin streaks.

'Sorry to bring it up, but I hear Elmo favoured you Mac, you lucky devil. It's your blond nut and pansy complexion that got her; why, why am I cursed with this ugly mug and lousy pelage?' He passed a hand over his meagre locks.

'You're jealous Dunst, it's my personality she's attracted to, more than anything else!'

'I've got another name for it,' he said gloomily in his rumbling voice. 'Do you know Mac, I've been crazy about that girl ever since the first day I saw her?'

'Not surprised. She gets a man like that,' said Sandy, mindful of that last passionate encounter with her.

'I confess, her contempt for me so infuriates me that I want to hurt her just as she has hurt me, but Fate is giving her a bad deal instead, now that her fiancé, or should I say financier, has been called to his Maker.' His eyes burned with a fire in their dark sockets. 'Did you know Elmo has disappeared?'

'Disappeared?' Sandy repeated, dumbfounded.

'Yes,' he said. 'Gone awa a y!' he boomed loudly, so that the remaining diners looked round in surprise. Those who knew Dunster only smiled and resumed their eating or talking.

'I can't believe it!' Sandy said, perturbed. 'Where on earth has she gone?'

'All I know is that the bungalow is shut up and for sale and the whereabouts of the couple are unknown.'

'Well, people don't just vanish in a place the size of Barbados. I'll ask Leo. He'll know where she's gone. That was damn quick!'

'Don't worry, she'll turn up by and by and with a bag of dough, if I know anything of Leila.'

Sandy ignored this remark.

'By the way,' he said fixing Thunder with his eye, 'How come you are toting Mrs Dare around?'

'Frankly,' said Thunder, 'I detest the woman but she gets me quite a bit of news for my paper one way and another. She clamps down on my wanting to blow the lid off the Obeah House though. She likes going there herself you see. She's a lousy woman, smokes marihuana and eats opium. A thorough bad lot and fornicates like the devil.'

160

'Does old Dare have any inkling of his wife's activities - or Maureen, for that matter?' Sandy asked, horrified at the thought of sweet Maur being privy to this sort of thing.

'I'm sure Dare does, but he wouldn't like an open scandal. Anyhow, he has a bird of his own. It's a good thing her stepdaughter has Granny to turn to. Incidentally,' he said, swivelling his dark eyes in Sandy's direction, 'You're a son of a bitch making love to the girl and having side lines like Lois Dance and Elmo! Blast it! Do you want all the women?'

'I don't want any of them. It's only experience I'm after.'

'Same here! Why do we go with women except for experience?' Thunder rumbled morosely. 'Hey! Isn't it time we had a drink? I need cheering up.'

With the main attraction, the fascinating Golden Girl away from the scene, the delights of the bars and dance-halls had lost both lustre and draw for Sandy so he edged away from his associates there and had another try at respectability.

The fleshpots of the Waterfront did without him while his life once more assumed a conventional routine for the nonce; a dinner at the house of one of the quieter-living Barbadians, a dance at Mr Pomcroy's attractive Marine Hotel or an evening of poker or Bridge comprised his after hours' life.

He spent more time with Maur at her Granny's, always strictly chaperoned of course. They were both pleased at his reformation and sometimes organised picnics to the part of the island called Scotland for its supposed resemblance to that country. This part, unlike the rest of the island was of volcanic rock and the result of some pre-historical cataclysm of nature so was hilly. The scenery and beaches were ideal for outings and whiled away some of his leisure time pleasurably enough.

Thus, quite a number of months passed with still no word or sign of Elmo. He still visited Aimée and Lois's on occasion where he was always sure of finding Lois ready for love, though he did have to tolerate some tempestuous scenes. Jansen was still being entertained by Aimée, so they had some jolly foursomes swimming and dining together.

ᴇ

Then Señor Luiz Mendoza arrived to ruffle the pool of tranquil labours at the Bank. This South American gentleman purchased a draft on the New York branch for $10 from Sandy, a circumstance however, that barely recorded itself on his mind.

One morning the Manager, accompanied by the Chief Cashier, went up to Sandy's desk looking extremely solemn. Had he issued a draft for $1,000 to L Mendoza? The name, but not the amount, registered and he referred to a copy of the bordereau of drafts issued on New York and there was Mr Mendoza - $10 not $1,000, May 1st.

'That, 'said the Chief Cashier, 'is what New York say. How do you explain that MacNeil?'

'Forgery,' said Sandy.

'Nonsense! Who forged it? Did you? Or have you been giving bank drafts away to South Americans?' distain and accusation in his voice.

That shook Sandy. No doubt about it now, he thought, the truth about his low associations must be common knowledge and now he was being unfairly and foully judged as a result. Nevertheless, he was enraged at the impunity.

The riddle was solved however, after some argument, correspondence and cabling New York, It transpired that the creative Mendoza had taken Sandy's $10 draft down to

Georgetown British Guiana where he had made the interesting alteration to $1,000.

He picked a Sunday when the banks were all closed, and having already struck up an acquaintance with a certain man of means, one Don Felipe in a hotel smoke room, asked this kind gentleman to advance him some cash on the draft. He wished to depart early on the Monday; alas, before the banks were open.

Such was the reputation of any English bank draft or cheque, that Don Felipe had no hesitation in letting the charming Señor Mendoza have the full amount in exchange for the bill. In due course the draft, paid into Don Felipe's account, reached the New York branch which refused to honour it, as the amount did not tally with Sandy's bordereau. Hence the agitation.

An expert was called in to examine the draft and found, after microscopical examination, that Sandy's writing had been neatly expunged and replaced by the new generous amount.

How was this done, they cried as one? It was found that it was easy enough to purchase a bottle of fluid that would erase without trace, any ordinary writing ink. From there on it was simplicity itself. The extraordinary thing was, that it had never been tried before. In a very short time, the Bank was issued with draft forms on a special paper that absorbed the ink right through to the back.

Sandy was further enraged as no apologies were forthcoming for the suspicion that he was the culprit. He began to seriously consider changing his occupation. Clamping his firm Scots jaw on several pertinent things he'd give much to say, he fulminated in silence and mentally rehearsed stunning them with a wealth of such sarcastic verbosity that he ended by restoring himself to his usual good humour.

❧ Chapter 17 ❧

Then she came back. He met Elmo again.

Bridgetown's mule-driven tram system made an infernal noise clattering along badly laid rails on the bare coral roads. The trams were open wooden contraptions with timber seats that ensured that you were liberally besprinkled with white coral dust if you were foolhardy enough to try this mode of transport.

Early one evening, finding his bike had a puncture but not being in the mood to deal with it, Sandy boarded one, on his way out to Hastings and dinner.

He found a vacant seat next to a girl in pale pink whose features were concealed beneath a large shady hat.

'Hello Sandy dear,' said a soft and familiar voice.

Sandy jumped. It was such a long time since he'd heard Elmo's husky contralto. He turned quickly and would have embraced her there and then had it not been so public.

'Great Scot, darling! Where did you spring from? How are you? Are you going to the bungalow? How's Leila? Is she with you?'

'One question at a time Sandy dear. It's a long story and won't improve in the telling, but if you care to come up tonight I'll give you all the lamentable news.'

Her voice had a sad cadence to it that it had lacked in former days. Sandy looked the beloved face. It was still beautiful he saw in the soft rosiness of the early evening light, but looked thinner and a little careworn, so that her exotic beauty now seemed refined by anguish. She appeared if anything, even more attractive.

'Are you back at the bungalow?'

'No, we had to sell it!' she said with a cynical laugh. 'We are now pigging it in a shack up in Timbertown with 'dem sugar cane folks,'.'

'Too bad!' he said, shocked at this news, 'but all the same, I'll come up after dinner if you tell me how to recognise your new abode.' He made to get up as the tram was nearing his stop near the Savannah.

'Look for the shack with the bright yellow door,' she said, 'Leila painted it herself so that people will find me easily,' she replied neutrally.

A chill passed over him as he took her hand in farewell with a repeated promise to see her later. So that's how it is, he thought wretchedly, as he walked up to the hotel. There's no more money so Elmo is again for sale.

Dunster was already seated at Sandy's favourite table with his drink in his hand.

'Why the abysmal gloom Mac? Lost a bob and found a tanner?'

As Sandy sat down, he told the boy who came for his order to bring him a double scotch and soda.

'Oh-ho! That's bad, Mac. Very unlike you to drink on an empty stomach. Must be serious!'

'Very funny ain't you,' replied Sandy. 'I just don't feel too cheerful tonight, that's all.'

'And I know the reason, dear boy. You've just seen Elmo and heard the sad news, I'll bet.'

'You know everything don't you?' Sandy grumbled. 'How the devil do you know I've seen her?' he asked, glowering.

'I don't. I guessed it. I heard to-day she was in town so I proceeded to make a few contacts in search of information and if you'll keep your hair on, I'll tell you all I know.'

'Carry on and tell me the worst,' sighed Sandy taking his drink from the tray proffered by the returning boy.

Dunster seized a fried chicken leg from his plate and after taking a swig from his drink, started to gnaw on it.

Sandy was convinced that his mode of eating was like his mode of living, simply exhibitionism. Possibly, he thought, he was so conscious of his weird appearance that he tried to divert attention from it by displaying other atrocious traits. To Sandy's mind, they merely exacerbated it. In his present mood it seemed more noticeable.

Flinging the gnawed bones onto his plate and taking a further swig, Dunster waved to the boy. 'Are you eating or sticking to the drink, old chap?'

'Well, I suppose I'd better eat, but your manners put a man off his food Thunder!' Sandy ordered food and turned back and further admonished his companion,

'Well, get on with the tale Thunder. The suspense is doing me no good.'

'It would appear she never left Barbados. She and Leila have been living concealed in the Obeah House while Elmo had her baby.'

'Wh..*what*!' Sandy ejaculated. 'Her baby? What baby?'

'Strange as it may seem, Elmo has had a baby and by its looks and colouration, the late lamented Ramon is the father.'

Sandy involuntarily drew a deep breath of relief as a rapid calculation set his mind at rest.

'Of course,' added Dunster grinning wickedly, 'it might be a throwback to her coloured ancestors!'

'Never mind the surmises,' he said irritably. 'What happened then?'

'As soon as she recovered from the physiological phenomenon of childbirth, she made up her mind to return to civilization, meaning Bridgetown. Funds were probably getting low and Leila needed convalescing.'

'Heavens! Don't tell me Leila's had a baby too?'

'Hardly, she's much past that, but she's had typhoid. It's endemic out at Black Rock.'

'Good God! Whatever next?' Sandy cried, horrified.

'Some old pal of Leila's let them have some rude habitation in Timbertown where they have settled pro tem, till things look up. I believe Leila has already painted the door yellow to attract prospective customers.'

'I know about the yellow door. Hell's Teeth! What an end to all Elmo's dreams of becoming one of the first ladies of Caracas.' Sandy said. 'Let's have another drink.'

Their meal at an end, Goops, finishing his meal at a nearby table, got up and came over to them, puffing on a newly lighted cigar.

'Am I wrong, or did I hear the name of our Obeah Priestess mentioned?'

'You did,' said Dunster. 'She has returned home with her baby.'

'*Das ist wundershon*, a baby! And who is the father? Our friend the Schottlander, our good friend Mac?'

'Could be, could be' said Dunster reflectively, 'only Mac is a Nordic blond and the baby is a Southern brunette.'

'*Ganz gut*, let us adjourn to Maxie's Bar and purchase something wherewith to baptise the head of the latest anthropological wonder, the product of conception between a Creôle Mamaloi and a South American Joe.'

'You have a horrible way of putting things Goops,' said Sandy, 'but by all means let us have a drink away from here.'

The three of them made their way down the hill and entered Maxie's Bar.

'Instead of being so damnably facetious about the girl in her dreadful fix, why don't you suggest something practical. Let's give her some money,' said Sandy irritably.

'Waste of cash, old chap.' Dunster replied. 'Neither Leila nor Elmo has any idea of the value of money. Leila would buy rum and Elmo a new frock or necklace. Corazon must have given them quite a lot of money from time to time. He was a generous bloke and what have they done with it? Blued it, just blued it.' adjured Dunster. 'If you are in an altruistic mood Mac, you could adopt the infant and keep it at the Bank!'

Sandy glared at him and turned his shoulder morosely, sipping his drink. He stood awhile at the bar in a sour mood while the other two talked in a bantering way that Sandy felt was done deliberately to annoy him.

A buggy drove up and deposited a customer at the door. On an impulse Sandy decided to take advantage of it and vigorously hailed the driver.

'Cheerio, you two sods. I'm off!' he said and took a flying leap into the vacated vehicle, shouting, 'Timbertown!' to the startled Negro on the box. Rude and sarcastic remarks followed him from the two in the doorway, coupled with warnings against sleeping with the tarts in shack town.

As they drove along the coast road his thoughts were of Elmo. The buggy rolled along, the sea as entrancing as ever with the moon's sheen on it; the surf pounded on the reef and hissed on the sand. The tropical flowers perfumed the air and washed over him in the cool breeze that blew off the Caribbean Sea. What in the world the girl was to do now, Sandy couldn't imagine. The thought of her degenerating into one of the habitués of the lower haunts on the quays, riddled with disease and sotted with cheap rum was too vile to contemplate.

He reflected ruefully on his own resolution to reform her and help rescue her from evil. He had done nothing. Now, he decided, he really must make an effort, but as usual was vague in his mind as to how the attempt could be made or the form it could take.

'Here you are sah, Timbertown,' said the cabby, drawing up to a wide track leading off the main road.

No need to announce it, thought Sandy, I can smell it! He paid off the cabby and made his way along a dusty and uneven road to the shanty town, a heterogeneous collection of wooden and corrugated iron shacks where the black population who worked on the sugar plantations were housed.

It was an unsavoury housing scheme and represented the white man's notion of giving freedom to the Negroes. The Negro had to shift for himself on poor wages and find his own domicile. The cane-workers chose Timbertown and lived freely there in dirt, drunkenness and squalor with other freedom-loving folk, toughs, thieves, prostitutes and even some respectable Negroes, who with the gregariousness natural to them, joined the happy band of shack-dwellers.

The sanitation was primitive and Timbertown smelled to high heaven but there was much music and much liberty, with a good deal of licence. He passed a bar where a noisy crowd were drinking and playing dice but not far along the way the door stood invitingly open to a Mission House. Another goodly crowd were outside it singing Moody and Sankey hymns with great fervour, led by a large fat Negro in a black frock coat.

Sandy stopped awhile, irresistibly attracted as always to Negro singing voices, as they poured out Ira Sankey's *'Come, come, Wanderer come, there's plenty for you in your Father's home,'* their liquid notes filling the night air. The black pastor, catching sight of Sandy's pale face, bawled out a welcome for him to enter, as all sinners, whether black or white, could be washed in the cleansing fountain of blood.

Sandy beat a hasty retreat. Blood, blood, he muttered. Always blood! Cock's blood, lamb's blood, always the same motif of the priests! No better than the Aztecs in their black bloodstained robes and long tangled hair wielding their knives of obsidian in their terrifying human sacrifices! Can't I find a religion without blood in it, he grated? He mentally shook himself and looked about to see if he could discover Elmo's new abode.

The shack town was built on a gently rising mound with a few huts at the base. As the ground rose, the buildings grew denser so that along the brow of the hill there was a confused string of lights from the windows of the huts.

There were native Bajans of every shade everywhere and nimble barefoot children, some in rags and some quite naked got among his feet begging for pennies. A baker's dozen of Negroes of both sexes accompanied him to Elmo's shanty although no direction was really necessary as he soon saw the yellow door lit up by a paraffin lamp hung above it.

He knocked and entered. A sickly air pervaded the ill-lit room. Elmo was seated on what Sandy recognised with a start, was the very divan from the Obeah House that he and Elmo had lain on together that night. It seemed so long ago.

He was shocked at sight of her dressed in an old wrapper. She was holding her baby rolled in a piece of blanket. He went over and looked down at the child. It was a sad, puny little thing with a yellow puckered face. With its eyes closed, it looked neither dead nor alive.

'She's been vomiting,' Elmo said softly. 'I don't think the goat's milk agrees with her and I can't feed her myself. I had milk but I didn't like the idea of her drinking from a breast with a snake on it so I put away the milk with belladonna leaves. She always seems to have the stomach-ache. She's so small,' she said sadly. 'It's because she came early. I wonder now if she'll live?'

Sandy couldn't find a word to say.

She laid the quiescent child down on the divan and sat listlessly, folding her hands in her lap. Sandy's heart smote him. He sat down on a stool and glanced round the room.

The place was untidy and frowzy, the corners filled with rubbish that had been swept from the centre of the room.

'Awful dump Sandy, isn't it? I wish I hadn't asked you up. Leila's always drunk now and makes no effort to tidy up and she used to be so particular,' she continued in the same quiet voice, presumably for the sickly babe's sake, only now it sounded dispirited. 'She's sleeping off a drunk now in the other room. Go in and see her. 'Go on, you'll get a surprise.'

He rose and pushed aside a dirty curtain and looked into the only other room. On a mattress was the wreck that was Leila.

Her hair, or what was left of it was white, the scalp showing through bald patches. Her face was pallid and emaciated and showed all the bones. Her frame, once so robust, was now gaunt and showed like a large skeleton through the thin grimy frock in which she lay.

'Good God! What's happened to the woman!' he cried in astonishment and dismay.

'Typhoid. She caught it at Black Rock. Her black hair came out and her flesh practically fell off her body,' replied Elmo.

The woman's mouth was open and a horrible drunken snoring issued from the throat. Of her fine white teeth, only a few were left.

'She's a sorry mess Elmo, but it's a judgement on her all the same.'

'Why a judgement on her especially Sandy?'

'Well, she didn't give you a square deal. She could have looked after you better than she did!' he said bitterly.

'Don't blame Leila,' she answered. 'It was all my own fault. I was saturated with that Obeah cult and knocked off my balance.'

'Why Elmo!' exclaimed Sandy, 'Have you given up the Obeah?'

'Completely. The one that you saw, was the last of my 'fits.' I now know it had something to do with my sex life. I feel more normal than I have ever done, but now I get fits of depression instead. I have terrible moods of melancholy as if I'm living in a vacuum.'

She rose and taking the sleeping child carried it into the other room. He watched her lay it on a corner of the mattress and realised how thin she had become. The beauty he had seen in her face on the tram seemed gone. Had it been the pink outfit, a trick of the light, he wondered? Was it on entering this dump with its squalor, the sick child and that drunken wreck of a woman that had leached away the attractiveness he had seen such a short while ago?

Elmo re-entered the room. She went over to a corner and rummaged among some clothes there and came back with an unopened bottle of whisky.

'I have to hide this from Leila. We may as well have a drink, there's nothing else to do,' she said, searching for glasses.

Sandy stood, confused and uncomfortable at the change in her. The vital personality and the exotic beauty that had drawn him like a moth to a flame was gone leaving only as far as he could see at the moment, a worn prettiness that struck him now as tawdry. The black arts that had absorbed and obsessed her, the demon possession, in their going had taken her vivid essence with it. She must have sensed something of his thoughts by his expression.

'You don't care for me now Sandy?' She passed him a tumbler with some whisky in it.

'No Elmo,' he said cruelly, by now disturbed and irrationally angry with her for getting him up here to witness all this degradation and squalor. 'There's nothing left of you. Where's that wonderful vital creature of wickedness I used to know? You've gone all ordinary dear.'

Looking at her, all he felt right now was indifference. Even worse, a faint contempt for her lack of grit. The bleak realization unnerved him even more. This subdued Elmo held no fire, no mystery now without the spice of wickedness and vivid sensuality. It was as if she was just a shell, the real substance just melted away.

He took a sip of his drink. 'And what's this?' He picked up a missal from the table. 'Taking up religion?'

'Father Timothy has been here. He talked, but failed to persuade me, but left that for me to read.' she replied. She looked at him consideringly. 'I see now that it was the evil in me that you loved, - no, fascinated you I think. I only really appealed to your baser nature dear,' she said resignedly. 'Perhaps you don't realise it yourself, but I believe it. You are only really attracted to the immoral and wicked side of life.'

'Yes, I do realise it, Elmo. I fight against it constantly,' he quipped. His tone was flippant but it was to cover the uneasy recognition of the unpalatable truth: he'd discovered the sybaritic side to his nature and enjoyed it. A taste for the base and sinful, its vitality and rebelliousness, and the tantalizing, exotic, dark mystery surrounding Elmo held far more interest for him. 'It must be something to do with my heredity. The Scots were always keen on the supernatural.'

'When we have anything bad in our make-up, we always blame it on heredity Sandy, but anything good we take all the credit for.'

'I see that your visit from Father Timothy has made you a bit of a philosopher dear. Pass the whisky Elmo and let's forget it.'

'Ok Sandy, let's get drunk. When I'm drunk, I feel less like suicide.'

But the alcohol failed to brighten them as Sandy became infected with Elmo's dejection, at all the changes in her, the dirty shack in which she chose to live with the sick kid and the drunken Leila. His soul revolted. Now, in place of the love or passion he had felt for her, he was filled with a mean pity.

She lay on her side on the divan, curled up awkwardly without a trace of her former elegance, her eyes glassy with the drink and looked sulkily and unhappily at him.

'You wouldn't care to love me now Sandy. I'm not even properly washed - where in this dump? It stinks. Yes, I'm a shell of my former self, but one thing and one thing alone mitigates my wretchedness. I am free of Obeah, free from demons and blood and - and *Beresford* .' She almost spat the name.

'Beresford?'

'Yes. He poses as an ordinary respectable Negro but he is an evil old man, a sorcerer, a witch doctor and a hypnotist. Thank God, he has given me up as no further use to Obeah. He only tolerated us while I was carrying in the hope that I might resume my 'fits', but when they didn't recur and I didn't respond to his hypnosis, he slung us out in a fury.'

'Did he get you a doctor when you were in labour?'

'No, Beresford sent an old midwife. It's a miracle I didn't go septic with her spells and smelly old herbs.'

A silence fell on the place. Sandy felt stupid with the drink he had consumed and drowsed in his chair. Meanwhile Elmo succumbed to fatigue and whisky and fell asleep.

He roused and looked across at the girl. He couldn't bear to look at her lying with her mouth partly open, clothes tousled and the new boniness of her limbs on view through the crumpled openings of the silk wrapper. He felt inadequate and impotent to help her. He had not been able to suggest a thing about her future, only get half-soused. What a bloody awful mess, he thought, and what a blithering idiot am I.

He got up quietly and let himself out of the shack, thinking miserably of the long walk he had ahead of him and wishing he'd thought to ask the cabby to come back for him. Timbertown was asleep except for a few stray lights. He stumbled down to the main road.

'Mistah Mac!' said the voice of Leo.

174

'Heaven bless you Leo!' Sandy cried fervently as he recognised Leo sitting in his sports car. 'How on earth did you know that I was here?'

'Went into Maxie's for a cigar and met Umpster Dumpster wid de German who mentioned you were probably wid Elmo.'

'Take me home Leo. I'm fed up. Gloomy as all hell.'

'Dat not like you Mistah Mac,' he said as he revved up the engine and sped along the road. 'but I know what yo' feel. Things bad, too bad for Elmo. She change since Corazon die; she change. No life now, all fun finish.'

'Yes, all fun finish Leo.' He lapsed into a depressed silence.

As he dropped Sandy off at the side gate to the bank, Sandy said desperately, 'Why don't you marry her yourself Leo and look after her! You know how she'll end if left to her own devices!'

'Mistah Mac, I love dat woman ever since I can remember, but she nevah listen to a black nigger like me. She kick me out. It no use Mistah Mac. No, she find her own way out of her trouble.'

'I suppose you're right Leo. And we can't do anything about it. Goodnight.'

'Goodnight sah.'

Sandy went into the Bank and mounted the stairs with no trace of joy in him.

❧ Chapter 18 ❧

War, and rumours of war filled the papers: the assassination of a Duke whose main pleasure was the killing of tens of thousands of birds on his game preserves: mobilization of armies. This was the news. More and more German nationals were passing through Barbados on their way home from South America.

As if already influenced by the uncertainty of life, the tempo of reckless living increased in Barbados and Sandy threw himself into nightly rounds of dancing and wild living. Germans were everywhere with plenty of South American money to spend, all in great spirits and talking openly of '*der Tag*', ready to go home determined to fight somebody, preferably the English.

Goops, and sometimes Dunster when he wasn't too busy with his paper, joined him in the night-life, especially with so many of his compatriots out on the town. He asked the German why he wasn't joining the nationals on their trek homeward, but he hedged; he had an English wife, or he was too old, or had been too long away from Germany.

He looked in vain for Elmo. He half-hoped he would see her again as she used to be, healthy, exotic, vital. Yet she stayed away. He knew that for him to return to shack town was a useless endeavour from his own inability to change anything, let alone witness it. He knew it was a cowardly retreat but he couldn't bear the change; he wanted life and fun.

Encountering Leo just before going out to Stafford House one evening, he asked after her. She was seldom seen outside her two-roomed shack with the yellow door, he said. She was heard quarrelling frequently with Leila, steadfastly refusing to entertain any visitors other than

Father Timothy whom she saw frequently, or Dr Kilcoyne, who did not think the baby would ever thrive in the atmosphere of that hut. Their money too was dwindling. Elmo was refusing all help, reiterating that she would take her own way out of her difficulties.

Take her own way out of her difficulties. He didn't like the sound of that phrase.

Goops, sitting at the table where he had joined Sandy and Dunster after their evening meal, looked up from the paper he was glancing over.

'*Ach, Donner und Blitzen, der Tag* approaches, *nicht war*?'

'Any moment now,' said Dunster. 'What I can't understand is what you are sticking around here for. You ought to be in Deutschland.'

'I don't know myself,' replied Goops, 'except Mrs Teufelmann refuses to leave here. In either case, it's too late now. Where are you two rascals off to tonight?'

'Well,' interjected Sandy, 'We were thinking of visiting an old friend of yours.'

'*Es ist gar nicht möglich,*' growled Goops. 'I have no friends, old or new.'

'He means Elmo.'

'*Himmel*! That's different! May I accompany you?'

'Certainly, 'said Dunster, 'Mac here says she's lost the best part of her looks and all her pep since she became a mother. I've forgiven her for being so lousy to me. I'll think I'll ask her to marry me.'

'A good idea Thunder,' agreed Sandy, 'I'll be your best man. First of all, let's take her some cash.'

'Let us adjourn to Maxie's Bar and discuss the situation,' suggested Goops.

Once in the bar however the other two settled down to drinking and discussing the political outlook. Sandy got restless and impatient as a booze session seemed to be developing, so ignoring their protests, he hailed a passing buggy and persuaded them to get in with him, but only after they had bought three bottles of Scotch 'to cheer up Leila and Elmo' as Dunster put it.

'By the way Thunder,' Sandy enquired, as the buggy finally got under way, 'What became of Ines who used to live upstairs at Maxie's?'

'Oh, she disappeared months ago with Rodriguez the Mexicano,' boomed Dunster. 'I quarrelled with her. One night I got annoyed with an article of domestic under-the-bed china and bunged it out of the window. It hit a wall and smashed to smithereens and she was very upset. It said 'A Present from Valparaiso' on it and held tender memories of its donor, one Francisco de Fererro y Quintana. I hate the things so I refused to replace it, so we parted in anger and reproach.'

'As you say in English, 'you put your foot in it',' smirked Goops.

'That's just what I did do; I'm always doing it, that's why I hate the things!'

The Professor then started getting sentimental and burst into song in a slightly off-key bass and sang '*Still wie die Nacht, still wie das Meer, soll meine Leibe sein.*' as the buggy rolled through the warm night.

As they drew near Timbertown, they caught the sound of Negro singing, swelling and filling the air with glorious sound.

'Hello! The whole town's '*en fête*' by the sound of it,' cried Dunster. 'There'll be plenty of rum tonight.'

'More like gin, I should say. They're singing Spirituals.'

'How right you are Mac!' he answered as they drew up at the dusty track leading to the village.

They paid off the driver, and with Sandy leading the way made their way slowly through the press of black humanity in the direction of Elmo's house.

'Hey you psalm-singing sods,' bawled Dunster. 'What's the fiesta?'

No-one answered him so they went on their way again, enveloped in a veritable reverberation of sound. They were followed by '*Swing low, sweet chariot, comin' for to carry me home,*' as they passed up the street. As they neared Elmo's hut they found some score of Negroes, both men and women, on their knees, hands clasped and harmonising the mournful melody.

The bright yellow door was shut. Sandy hesitated before entering.

'The baby is probably dead,' he said turning to the other two. 'I'd better knock.' He turned back and knocked rather hesitantly on the wooden door. No-one answered. They waited uncertainly for a moment.

'Come on,' said Dunster impatiently and pushed open the door.

With one accord, they all followed each other in and stopped on the threshold in shock. The scene before them impressed itself indelibly on Sandy's mind. He stood with his hand in his pocket grasping the money which they had subscribed together, some nine or ten pounds but a glance at the central figure told him there was no use for it now.

A frightful pang tore at his chest; Elmo lay, apparently unconscious, on the divan, her face very pale, her heavy-lidded eyes closed, the lovely nose pinched, her long chestnut hair in wild disorder on the pillow.

His breath caught in his throat. He was stunned.

Dr Kilcoyne was seated in a rickety chair in his shirt-sleeves smoking a cigarette. He looked up at their entry but said nothing. Sandy crossed over to the still figure and as he did so, something crunched underfoot. He looked down to see a number of Elmo's yellow flowers and their little green apples. He turned to the Doctor.

'What has happened?' he asked, voice abraded with emotion.

The Doctor bent down and picked up a sprig of the small apples and twirled them between his fingers.

179

'I surmise she has been eating these,' he replied. 'They contain some toxic substance, a cardiac depressant. I have washed out the stomach,' he indicated a basin of greenish fluid, 'and injected a stimulant, but her passing seems to me to be a matter of minutes.'

The other occupant of the room had his back to them at the head of the divan and was engaged in lighting two candles on a small table that was covered by a white cloth. It was Father Timothy. A glass bowl beside the candles presumably contained holy water thought Sandy. The priest intoned softly in Latin. Sandy stood helplessly by the unconscious girl, too cut to the heart to do more than glance at her now and then.

'And so,' said the Professor, who had found himself a box to sit on. 'The Middle Ages appear with bell book and candle to exorcise the devil and prepare the soul of the pagan priestess for purgatory.'

Father Timothy turned. 'Professor Teufelmann, *surely shalt thou be ashamed and confounded for all thy wickedness.*'

'Quotation from my favourite author, Job,' muttered Dunster looking for somewhere to set the three bottles of whisky.

'This poor sister,' continued the priest quietly, 'sent for me before she committed this rash act, but I arrived too late to prevent her. She has repented of her sins and expressed a wish to enter Holy Mother Church again. Before she fell unconscious, I heard her confession and absolved her.'

'Then there will be a nice little competition when she meets her Voodoo gods and your plaster saints in Hell, Herr Friar!' said Goops, his deep guttural voice in harsh contrast to the gentle Irish one.

'Hey you two!' said Dunster who was leaning against a wall trying to prise the top off a whisky bottle with a penknife. 'Cut out the theological argument. Hell!' he exploded, as the penknife broke. 'This damn thing's on too tight.'

Sandy looked over at Dunster. He suspected he was dramatising, as he wasn't as drunk as he was pretending. It was a cover to hide his true feelings as he kept making furtive glances at the divan and his eyes looked suspiciously wet. He fumbled ineffectually at the bottle with trembling hands.

The door to the other room slowly opened and a bent old hag appeared holding a bundle in her arms.

'Shut up your bloody row Thunder and Lightning. You'll wake the baby.'

'Jeez! It's Leila,' he growled. 'What the hell happened to you?'

'I've been sick. I caught Typhoid. *Beaucoup de malade*.'

Still holding the unopened bottle, Dunster went over to peer at the woman.

'What a judgement on you Leila! What a judgement! You look a bloody hundred years old!'

'Sure,' said Leila, 'I feel it too. Here Mac, hold the kid while I get some glasses,' and she put the tiny bundle into Sandy's unwilling arms. Luckily the babe didn't wake. He stood there, nonplussed and feeling foolish. Leila went into the back room again in search of glasses, shuffling and feeble like a very old woman.

'A typical daddy!' observed Dunster drily as Sandy stood awkwardly holding the little bundle. 'but the bairn's complexion lets you out Mac. That's a combination of Venezuelan and Haitian, I'd say.'

Sandy sat down uncomfortably on a nearby stool holding the child and overcome by a feeling of uselessness and depression. He resented Goops sitting smoking disinterestedly. He resented Dunster and his bottles and he resented the doctor sitting back, bored and waiting for the end and probably pre-occupied with thoughts of his bed or some other patient. Why the devil hadn't he sent her to the

General Hospital? Was she too far gone for that? What a manner of dying for the Golden Girl, he thought savagely, surrounded by a bunch of incompetent fools and drunks!

A low groan drew his attention to the divan. To his relief Elmo's eyes opened. Seeing Sandy nearby holding the baby brought a little smile to the tortured mouth. Getting up, he bent over her to let her see her child, but the Doctor pushed him gently to one side and placed his stethoscope over her breast to listen to her heart.

After listening for a while, he straightened himself. He stepped back and shook his head. He signed to Sandy to show Elmo her baby. He bent over her once more and the fevered eyes seemed to express her gratitude. Then in an almost imperceptible voice, she spoke.

'I -I can hardly see you! - Ah, your gold hair, yes, - Sandy, - I forgot I had something to live for - my baby - too late now...'

Father Timothy stood beside him with an anguished expression on his face that echoed Sandy's silent distress. Elmo whispered. 'Father - baptise my baby.'

'The baby is already baptised Elmo,' he replied trying to smile at her.

'Thank you - both,' she whispered breathily.

Leila was standing with her back against the wall by a rickety table on which she had set out the glasses and Dunster's bottles. Sandy went over to her and handed her the infant and went back and going onto his knees beside her, took Elmo's hand, looking at the doctor to see if he had any objection, but he slowly nodded his head in assent. Her great eyes held him in an all-embracing look, while with an effort she lifted her other hand, placing it on his hair, which she smoothed once or twice. A puzzled expression settled on her face and she raised herself slightly, peering closely at him. He put his free arm behind her to support her, when a startled cry escaped her, making him jump and startling the others.

'Sandy! I think I'm going blind. I can't see you!' A spasm shook her frame, her heavy lids closing as if in resignation. Her body relaxed as he allowed it to sink back onto the pillows. There was no sound or movement in the room while everyone seemed to wait expectantly for the end. In a little while, a dread and unpleasant sound heralding death, came from her throat. It only lasted a moment and with a last sigh, Elmo's body stilled. Sandy had a fleeting impression that he saw her spirit leave. Sorrowfully, seeing the sudden blankness in the once beautiful face, he gently released her hand and silently sat back awkwardly on the stool beside her, feeling hopelessly inadequate and wretched.

The suspended silence with broken by the priest's softly spoken Latin phrases.

Dr Kilcoyne rose leisurely and automatically put his fingers on Elmo's pulse.

'Finis. The end,' he murmured.

Leila stood, the baby in her arms wrapped in its little blanket, tears rolling down her raddled cheeks. But no sobs issued from her throat. The Professor sat on his box, his elbows on his knees, his fingers entwined, the inevitable cigar between his teeth. His face was in shadow so Sandy could not discern his expression. Dunster stood with arms folded, looking as lugubrious as a mute and glancing expectantly at the whisky bottle. The Doctor was packing his bag preparatory to leaving.

'I expect there will be an inquest,' he said, addressing Leila, 'but you'll hear about that later; probably tomorrow. Goodnight, Father Tim,' he continued and made for the door, 'and a good night to you my friends,' he said giving them all a comprehensive look of antipathy. He went out, shouting to someone to fetch his carriage.

Father Timothy was reciting the offices for the dead and sprinkling holy water while trying to keep his composure under the sardonic gaze of the grinning professor. The priest looked intensely sad thought Sandy and more affected than anyone.

'My dear *Donner und Blitzen*,' said Goops at length, turning to Dunster. 'Pour out a drink for the company, we are getting gloomy.'

Dunster willingly and hastily complied, handing out drinks all round but he refrained from including the priest. Leila, her glass of whisky in her hand, stood by the bed watching either the cleric or looking wretchedly at the wreck of her ward Elmo. God knows what thoughts occupied her mind.

Grasping Sandy and Dunster by the elbows, Goops steered them into a corner where they continued drinking, Sandy at any rate to numb his feelings.

'Do you know why the Herr Friar looks so miserable?' the professor whispered harshly. 'I'll tell you. It's his Christian conscience. He killed her.'

'Herr Goops, you're drunk!' said Dunster.

'I don't mean he is directly responsible for her death,' he continued more audibly, 'but he contributed to it. Didn't he get her fired from that convent of hers because his libido was stirred to cracking point by Elmo's exhibitionism? To save his soul he got the Mother Superior to expel Elmo on the grounds that she was corrupting the girls when it was himself that was being corrupted! I contend that if he had followed his natural instincts and made love to the girl, she would still be alive!'

'What rot, Professor,' said Sandy tiredly, 'you know as well as I do that he is an avowed celibate. Leave it alone!'

Goops pulled down his mouth and merely looked sardonic. He broached the second bottle. Sandy suddenly had a strong desire to burst into tears. Dunster was swaying on his feet and began to sing quietly in a maudlin way, '*Brief life is here our portion.*'

Dunster hiccupped breaking off his melody.

184

'That's a horrible song, Herr Donner, you sound like a Baptist.'

'C'rect. Baptist, corn and bread, Herr Goops! You know everything!'

Sandy ignored them in a kind of dulled indifference.

An agitated knocking came at the door, which Sandy hastened to answer. It was Leo, hatless, his face shining with sweat.

'Mistah Mac! De Doctor didn't tell us one thing 'bout the sickness! Is it Elmo?'

'Yes Leo. She's dead. Poisoned herself with Manchineel.'

'Dead?' he cried, aghast at the news. 'Dead?'

With startling rapidity, the word echoed from lip to lip of the natives assembled at the door, until the whole of Timbertown must have heard it. Leo turned to the suddenly vast concourse of Negroes who had gathered rapidly and silently in minutes.

'Sing niggers! Sing!' he cried and led them in his robust tenor to sing the Lord's Prayer as the West Indians harmonise it, the entire crowd taking up the melody.

'Great,' said Dunster coming outside to listen, 'That satisfies my soul, that does.'

'A bellyaching noise, I call it,' grunted Goops, following him. 'Why don't they sing something cheerful? Superficial Negro emotions! They don't mean a thing. Give them Obeah and they'll have the same sensations! Distract their attention with some other incident and they'll forget their grief.'

'For God's sake, *shut up* Goops,' said Sandy tiredly.

As the voices came to the Amen and a silence followed, they became aware of the thunder of a heavy horse's hooves on the coral road and ever and anon a raucous shout and the clanging of a bell. All heads turned in the direction of the Worthing road from whence the rider was bellowing some message.

'It's One Eye Dan on his horse!' cried one old man 'and he's tellin' some news, some big news!'

Sandy's mind flew to Dan's efforts on the death of Queen Victoria. The rider came galloping nearer, waving his huge hand-bell and thundering up the track to Timbertown. One-Eyed Dan, for of course it was he, reigned in the big horse and in a stentorian voice roared.

'Bajans all! Dis midnight England declare war on Germany! God Save de King!'

After making the announcement twice, he gave the animal a resounding thwack and wheeling the sweating beast, tore off back to the road, clanging his bell and roaring out at intervals until the sound dwindled away into the night.

After a moment's stunned silence, the assembled crowd, with loud whooping and dancing and singing of 'God Save the King,' and consigning all Germans to perdition, gave themselves over to this fresh news, all thoughts of Elmo's death eclipsed by this astounding intelligence.

'What did I tell you,' said the Professor, looking sourly at the mob. 'As unstable as water.'

'Goops!' said Dunster with a wicked grin, 'We're now at war with you! Would you prefer to be shot now, or later?'

'*Ach Gott, nicht scheissen*, I'm an old man and a good friend of England. They'll intern me at the worst.'

'That remains to be seen,' said the newspaperman. 'Suppose you are a German spy? You'll probably be shot at dawn.' His dark eyes gleamed mockingly.

The German grew livid.

'Herr Dunster, I do not think that remark is in very good taste!' He looked really annoyed and Dunster gave Sandy a significant look as if to say that perhaps he'd hit the nail on the head.

'I must go to my wife,' said Goops.

'And I must go to the Office, otherwise I'll get the sack,' rumbled Dunster. 'Got your car Leo?'

186

'Yes sah, Mistah Dunster, down de road. If you an' de Professor go down, I be wid you shortly.'

As the two enemies moved off, Leo and Sandy went back into the shack to have a last look at Elmo.

Leila had washed her and combed her hair so she looked composed, and momentarily to Sandy, sadly beautiful. Moving closer he saw that this was an illusion. There was no-one there, Elmo had subtly gone; the face was waxy and empty and he was struck heavily by the hard reality of her death. He felt an unaccustomed dismay and didn't want to account for it.

He noticed that Leila had folded Elmo slim hands on her breast. They held a crucifix, put there by the priest he guessed but Sandy felt they should have held her favourite Manchineel flower.

Leo was blubbering softly.

'Wait till Beresford heah dis!' he said thickly, 'He make big palaver at Black Rock,' his dark face unashamedly wet with tears.

Sandy looked briefly again at the shell that had been Elmo. Golden Girl. He reflected miserably on the terrible waste of it all. A young, beautiful and highly intelligent girl destroyed, her whole life saturated with black superstition, and the evil and heredity that had brought her to this pass. He pushed aside the unwelcome reminder of Elmo's prophesy for Ramon. Why the hell hadn't Ramon married her first? Was her beauty all that mattered to him too, he thought, on a fresh spurt of anger and shame? Anyway, he couldn't bear his thoughts any more. He looked at Father Timothy.

He sat at the head of the divan holding a rosary in his hands and some devotional book he was reading. His curly black hair was already tinged with grey and he looked incredibly sad and troubled as he sat there with his head bowed. Sandy placed a hand on his shoulder in sympathy.

He looked up,

'I overheard what that infernal German said about me, but it's a lie. My love for this poor child was pure. It was her soul I sought, not her body. I believe now I have saved her soul for eternal life.'

'I believe you have Father Tim,' said Sandy. 'It is certain that had she lived, your task would have been well-nigh impossible. Who's to say Obeah and prostitution wouldn't have slowly destroyed her?'

With Leo before him, Sandy walked out of the shanty slowly shutting the door behind him and with the gesture he felt as if he'd shut out a portion of his life that he had not fulfilled.

They walked down to the car, Leo silent and miserable. There they found Goops and Dunster in heated argument about who was responsible for the war.

The effects of the alcohol were wearing off and the events of the night combined to fill him with a profound depression. He got in beside Leo, who quickly got into high and stepped on the gas. The resulting wind blew away the last fumes of the whisky and the calm peace of the tropic night made thoughts of war too incredible to contemplate or to envisage the carnage and grief that was to follow.

'What are your plans, Mac?' said Dunster at last.

'Going home pronto to join up. What about you?'

'I don't think I'll be able to go pronto, just like that. The paper won't release me immediately but I hope to get over to England in time to be in at the death.'

At that, all the occupants of the motor fell silent as they drove through the balmy night back to the lights of Bridgetown.

❧ Chapter 19 ❧

As Lieutenant Alexander MacNeil, he had reached Ouderdom in Belgium at nightfall, where 'Details,' the clearing house for his unit, was situated. He was rejoining his battalion after his second spell in hospital from shrapnel and bullet wounds and like many other junior officers reporting at 'Details' he was regarded as a bit of a nuisance.

He knew of old that those hanging on to jobs behind the lines were happiest when these subalterns were moving up to the Salient, where, they thanked God, they never heard of them again. The lead-swingers at 'Details' were never quite at ease in the presence of the Poor Bloody Infantry about to take the road to 'Wipers.'

Sandy found there was the usual difficulty about sleeping accommodation, for everyone was well-housed bar the itinerant Subaltern. He was told he might kip down in his flea-bag on the floor of the mess after that establishment was closed if he liked. Sandy didn't like and finding that the C. of E. Chaplain had a large tent to himself, he meekly suggested he might share it. The chaplain flatly refused, how was he to know, he protested, that Sandy didn't have vermin? Sandy, silently fuming, returned to the mess. He found out there that the man never went to the front line; there was very little chance of him ever being infested with lice. Pity! he thought tiredly. A nice infestation would improve his Christianity no end.

Sitting down gloomily in the mess, he ordered a drink. The place was full of lead-swingers, he observed sourly. He'd heard somewhere that it took eight men behind the lines to keep one man in the trenches and he could well believe it, looking around him.

His destination was a part of the line facing Kemmel Hill, a tough spot they said, no trenches, just funk holes and very wet. But at any rate, he thought, at least I'll find men after my own heart.

'Can't I get up there tonight?' he asked a red-faced obese Major, who had, thought Sandy from experience, all the signs of an N.C.O. raised from the ranks.

'Yus,' he said, 'if you bloody-well like to take the bloody transport with you.'

'Alright then. I don't mind. I'll take the transport, but what about the Transport Officer?'

'He's bottled. Sleepin' it off in his tent. You'll have a couple of N.C.O.'s with you to show you the road.'

'Any possibility of getting a word with the Transport Officer, or is he too blotto?'

'Try him. I'll get a bloke to show you his tent,' and the fat Major sent for a man, the type Sandy often found at 'Details' and base camps, the operative word being base. This one was a white-faced rat who had been swinging the lead for years and looked it.

'Come on you,' Sandy snarled in the charming way he had learned after nearly four years of war. He had lost any illusions he might have possessed. With his Division, he had moved around many parts of that long line of slaughter called The Western Front and found that aside from all the trench soldiery, there existed many men who executed dangerous, horrible and painstaking work while a great mass of others were dodging the column in every conceivable capacity; from ranks, to Sandhurst deadheads at H.Q. and public school wallahs wangled into Brigade appointments. Here was another of those frightened rabbits he thought bitterly, eyeing his guide with a disillusioned eye; frightened rabbits scared of the death they'd never die but glad, oh so glad, to shove others in their places to suffer, be cut about by shrapnel and to die so that they might live. Twice he'd been badly wounded and had spent time in hospitals in Craigleith, Edinburgh and in Ensleigh Palace in London and had seen men suffer, and die too, there, as well as in the field. At 28, Sandy was a confirmed cynic. His experiences had warped and dulled his mind and deadened his feelings, the only things that mattered were food and drink and sleep.

So here he was having his third go and at the Salient, of all places, he thought. They're determined to kill me off this time. He had a hunch he was going to get a 'packet' - and he did; at the attack on Kemmel Hill in August - 'penetrating wound of the lung,' the M.O. called it.

'Here you are sir,' said the white-faced rat, opening a tent flap. 'I'll leave you the light,' he added, passing Sandy the lantern he was carrying.

'Bugger off!' Sandy growled in the gentle manner of the war Subaltern.

Entering the tent, he shone the light upon a recumbent figure in a sleeping bag. He gave the mass a good shove with his boot,

'Wake up. Rise and shine you old sod-pot!'

'Cud-deah,' boomed a bass voice and to Sandy's utter astonishment, the awful head of Thunder and Lightning protruded itself from the kapok. He was now quite bald, pale, drawn and hideous but to Sandy, the sight of that old familiar mug was as gladsome as the Spring. He was delighted. They were both delighted. Dunster jumped to his feet, clad in a woollen vest and long pants and embraced Sandy fervently. He actually wept and then sat down violently on his kapok and rummaged in his kit. He eventually unearthed a bottle of whisky.

'Listen Dunst, I'm mighty pleased to see you, that goes without saying, but you seem to be the Transport Officer in this dump and I'm taking your place tonight.'

'So, they think I'm too blotto to take up the Transport, do they?' he boomed, and reached for his breeches.

191

'Dear old Dunst, I'll have a drink with you, several in fact, but please, do not prevent me from taking up the transport tonight. I must get up the line and meet my pals. I can't stick your column-dodging swine here a minute longer!'

'Mac, I can't blame you. They are appalling *schweinhunde* as old Goops would say; you remember old Teufelmann? Here, find a pew, sorry no seats. Squat down and have a snort.'

In a tin cup and the lid of a dixie, they shared their drink.

'So, you're a bloody transport Officer Dunst?'

'You've said it Mac! No other bloody good. Can't shoot, no idea of discipline! All I can do is lead a horse or wait for the horse to lead me. You make me feel lousy, you with your pretty medal ribbons and gold wound stripes,' he said rolling an eye over Sandy's uniform. 'But you Scotchmen thrive on war.'

'Dry up old man and tell me about Barbados. What happened after I left?'

'Plenty Mac. Goops got shoved into an internment camp and after the Belgian atrocities exposure, he was very badly treated, finally landing in the hospital. I tried to visit the old sod, but, no sand.' He topped up their drinks and settled back again.

'Maureen's father emigrated with his family to Pasadena, California.'

'Why?'

'No idea Mac. He just followed the lead of some Bajans who got scared and up sticks. Aimée and Jansen got spliced at the Registrars. I was there and had a tidy few. Lois wept and got silently stewed. Your name cropped up frequently with regrets at your silence. Jansen decided to go back to America where it was safer; - you know they were too proud to fight until thoroughly frightened. Later, Lois went and got engaged to an American Sergeant. The Sergeant duly got pneumonia and died in an army camp. Lois, free now, joined the chorus of the Chu Chin Chow show on tour and when that fizzled out, got a job as a telephone operator. After that, silence.'

'Good God! Why didn't they write to me?'

'You left no address, my friend, neither did you write, you blighter. You seemed to cut yourself off from everybody when you left Barbados.'

'Can't explain it old bean, except that I was a bit sick about things and all I wanted was to 'dree ma wyrd'[1] as they say in Scotland and 'dree'd' it I have, in all conscience.'

An N.C.O. appeared at the tent flap.

'Transport all present and correct Sir.'

Sandy got up.

'Cheerio, Dunst old man,' he said and shook his hand, 'I'm off.'

'God bless you Mac,' he said, now wrapped in a British Warm decorated with canteen medals, and wobbling on his pins. 'Mind that nag of mine, she's a bit nervous. Next time I'm up the line, I'll dig you out!' He put a hand on Sandy's shoulder. 'Mac, you're going up to one hell of a place as you know. Keep your head down. Great guys you Scotch, good show Mac, good show. I feel a bit unworthy; unworthy Mac.'

'Don't be a bloody fool Dunst. I wouldn't have your job for a million. The sergeant tells me its 12 miles to the Brigade and shelled half the way.'

'Bung ho, Mac,' said the haggard man, standing at his tent flap.

'Bung ho Dunst,' Sandy said and followed the N.C.O. to where a long line of transport stood awaiting its Officer.

---

[1] 'follow my own fate/destiny'

❧ *Epilogue* ❧

The two Tommies who were staggering through the heavy muck carrying the bloodied unconscious man on a stretcher, paused for a breather.

' 'ere, - 'arold! Looks like 'e's a gonner, or will be soon poor tyke. Wotcher say we take a break for a fag while we got the chance, eh?'

'Yeah, don't like the looks of 'im at all. My bleedin' back's killin' me any way. Leave the blighter 'ere. If he's still alive when we've 'ad a smoke, we'll trot 'im up to the medics then!'

'Righto chum. Can't stand bleedin' officers any rate,' and the two soldiers dumped the stretcher down on the churned up track and cast themselves down several yards away under the shade of a straggling hedge.

Through a dim haze, Sandy had heard this exchange and a white-hot anger boiled in his wounded chest. Struggling up onto one elbow, he scrabbled at the clots of blood filling his mouth from his punctured lung, coughed harshly and summoning up all the strength of his hardy Highland ancestors, bellowed in a stentorian voice to match One-Eyed Dan's, 'Get the bloody sodding hell back here, you filthy swine!' and sank back exhausted, gasping bloodily for breath as the startled Tommies flung down their fag-ends and scrabbled to their feet.

'Bleedin' 'ell Bert, oo'd 'ave thought it?' and they scurried back down the rutted lane. With one accord, they hoisted the stretcher and hastened off trying to avoid the blazing gimlet eye of the wounded man, which every now and then opened as Sandy fought to remain conscious till the field hospital was reached.

Post Scriptum

Sandy survived the war, still carrying bits of shrapnel around in him and spent two years in Paris studying art, before going on to become a doctor.

Goops died in hospital and thanks to his wife, received the last rites.

Thunder also survived the war and went back to his paper in Barbados and undeterred, took up his previous life style as soon as he possibly could.

9 781917 293037